**LEFT**

# LEFT
## TERRAN INCOGNITA
## BOOK 1

## PAUL MCGRATH

Published by

Stoney Creek Publishing Group

StoneyCreekPublishing.com

Copyright © 2025 by Paul McGrath. All rights reserved.

ISBN: 978-1-965766-02-6
ISBN (ebook): 978-1-965766-03-3
Library of Congress Control Number: 2024926226

No part of this book may be reproduced in any form or by any electronic or mechanical means, including information storage and retrieval systems, without written permission from the author, except for the use of brief quotations in a book review.

This book is a work of fiction. Names, characters, places, and incidents are either the product of the author's imagination or are used fictitiously, and any resemblance to actual persons, living or dead, business establishments, events or locales is entirely coincidental.

Cover design by Ken Ellis

Printed in the United States

*For my mother, who pushed me to read, and my wife, who pushed me to write.*

# CHAPTER 1

"**G**IRGACH! M'ACH SHEEROK! GIRGACH ZUNGIN! M'ACH GRADDAKH NIMNULES!" Every obscenity he had forsworn never to repeat rolled repeatedly off his tongue. But sometimes the cruder southern American vulgarities were more suitable for a given moment, he thought. This was one of those moments.

"Fuckfuckfuckfuckfuckfuckfuckfuckfuck. Fuckity-fuck fuck."

He had hurried as best he could, given the roads and the limitations of his vehicle. Roy stepped out of his navy-blue electric combo moped/bike, now parked on the side of the road, and surveyed the field. The scooter was excellent for negotiating the tight spaces of rural thoroughfares and paths, but a champion of the highways it would never be. The August Mississippi sun created heat mirages in the distance. A subtle wind whispered through the high grass, which was almost too sun-whipped to move. A choir of cicadas marked the moment with their melodic staccato. Or were they laughing?

He looked at his specialized watch. "Yeah, these are the right coordinates," he said to no one. "Now, where are they?"

He had rarely been this angry; strong emotions were discouraged among his kind. But it was an anger more directed at himself than at other parties. Yes, he was late. He knew it. Roy set his moped on its side, attempting to provide a modicum of concealment from the high grass and began searching the field for an answer he already had.

The broad field wound left around a peninsula of dogwoods and silverbells that extended from the dense woods. A pair of Florida maples stood like gallant watch towers amid the wild undergrowth. Just past this sentinel stand, the field became expansive, although much of it was shielded by the trees from road-weary eyes. Roy trudged through the field, taking care to avoid the plentiful fire ant mounds. Grass burrs began to collect on his shoes and jeans.

After a quarter mile or so, he found what he suspected—a circular section of grass that had surrendered to the weight of a large vessel. At the center, small scorch marks from the firing of a hyper-drive engine.

*They were here. Right here. And they left me*, Roy said to himself, gazing skyward. *No warning. No message. Nothing. Nimnules!* He followed that by mixing his vulgarities. *Fricking nimnules!*

Roy sat down on some leftover fenceposts and tore a long blade of grass. He smoothed it between his right thumb and forefinger as he thought. He put the grass partway into his mouth and played his tongue over it. *What now?* he thought.

For a moment, the fiction that was Roy McDonald receded into the recesses of his mind. Thinking like Roy wouldn't ease the pang of desperation echoing in his gut. He had to think like Anton, his birth name.

More specifically, Anton-7, a third brevet Centurion Guardian for Xylodon's Security Corps, his planet's elite service organization for military and law enforcement functions.

By Xylodonian regulations, the ship and its crew were right to leave. Anton knew it. The window for Earth departure was rather narrow at this time of year, and he was more than an hour late. He also knew that he had been friends, or at least collegial, with Termas-3 and Zephyra-9, his surveillance team companions, for years. Since before flight school. *Why couldn't you wait? Whatever the reason, it better have been a good one*, he thought.

It had been years since he had been home enjoying the warm,

# CHAPTER 1

soothing winds of Xylodon. Being an undercover operative on a foreign planet brought constant stress; the smallest mistake could bring an entire network crashing down. Earth was not the only planet under observation, but it was among the youngest and most promising—and the most dangerous. Anton had borne the stress of a secret life over multiple tours, largely combatting the snow and arrogance of the Northeast United States. Xylodon had its cold regions, but those never froze; snow did not exist.

But he still longed to prop his feet up in his reclusive cabin on Xylodon, sip a good *schnurberry* wine and gaze at his planet's three moons. He closed his eyes and thought of grilling *chorgats* caught in a nearby stream. He no longer had close relatives—his maternal and paternal had died not long after he graduated from the Protectorate Academy—nor did he have any matrimonial entanglements. Such freedom had its positives. But he still felt an attachment to his home world and his comrades.

The grass blade on his tongue turned as sour as his mood. Anton spat it out. He tried to look forward but found himself stuck in the present. Self-recrimination began to arrive like waves on a shore. Mississippi was a welcome change of pace, with its warming sun, blissful ignorance, and do-as-you-want attitude. The waters of the Gulf Mexico were a wonder to feel and behold, and within easy reach.

*Why am I always the late one,* he scolded himself. *Why am I always distracted by humans and their creations or excreta? And what was it this time? Waffle Barn.*

All bad things begin with Awful Barn, Anton sighed, remembering what he overheard one human saying. That bit of sarcastic wisdom did him little good at the moment, and he could not stay in this field forever.

He got up and plodded sullenly toward his moped.

# CHAPTER 2

OK, maybe not all blame extended to Waffle Barn per se, but its never-ending coffee pot contributed. Most Xylodonian agents—nearly all of them bearing a Centurion Guardian rank similar to Anton's—developed a fondness for the steaming Earth beverage. As there was nothing like it on Xylodon (think *xylophone* as a pronunciation guide), it was a favorite smuggling item.

No, this time Anton's late arrival could only be half-blamed on the café. It had more to do with Ezra "Gator" Hopkins. Ezra, now ninety-seven years young, was the self-proclaimed patriarch/savior/historian of Eudora, Mississippi. Eudora, home to about four hundred human souls, was named for author Eudora Welty, who earned herself a Pulitzer Prize for "The Optimist's Daughter" and a bushel of other awards for what also poured from her pages.

There is not much around and not much to see in Eudora. What Eudora has in abundance is a whole lot of nothing, along with uncaring eyes and tight lips, which made it the perfect location for Anton's third two-year tour on Earth. He and Termas and Zephyra lived in an RV park on the outskirts of Eudora. Whenever anyone asked about the strange, humming antenna arrays atop their RV,

## CHAPTER 2

they would just reply: "They are for streaming services. Very expensive, so the government pays for it."

It was an answer that brought envious nods instead of more questions.

Anton's previous tours had taken him to various spots in the Northeast U.S. and then to rural Arizona. That was the Xylodonian way: Send three-person teams to different points of nearly every Earth nation. Of course, countries like Somalia and Yemen rarely, if ever, made the list. Not even Xylodonians gave a shit about Somalia and Yemen. Also, any country ending in "stan" generally received a similar latitude; those countries were akin to Xylodon's Stone Age.

There had been close calls in his human interactions, of course, while stationed in the northeast regions of the United States. Once, some humans had knocked on his apartment door and he had opened it reflexively, forgetting to turn off his computer screen. A trained eye would have found the images quite interesting, but fortunately these humans were Girl Scouts peddling a variety of sweet treats and much more interested in coins than computers. He was able to dispatch them after buying six boxes of Thin Mints.

Then there was the night he drove his team's utility vehicle into a traffic stop set up on a country road in New Hampshire and found himself trapped within a gantlet of red and blue flashing lights. He searched his rearview mirror for a possible retreat but that was cut off by a station wagon with two baby carriers and a Saint Bernard hanging happily out the passenger window.

There was a tap-tap on his window, and Roy-Anton could see a shape through the condensation on the glass. He rolled down the window to reveal a young New Hampshire state trooper in a dark olive tunic and wearing the traditional "Smokey Bear" hat.

"Good evening, officer. Is there an accident up ahead?"

"No, sir. We got a state prison inmate on the loose. A killer. Broke out of the Concord pen," the trooper said. "Can I see your driver's license please?"

Oops. His team had forgotten to create that form of identification. "Sure thing, officer." Roy went through the motion of reaching around to his back pocket. "Oh, no," he said. "I must have left my wallet on the counter. I never do that. I'm so sorry. Officer, my name's Roy McDonald, and I'm with a Department of Agriculture team in Hillsboro. I was headed over to Manchester to bring back some takeout. See, they gave me cash," Roy said, holding up some green bills.

"So, you're a fed, are you," replied the trooper. "Well, Mr. Fed, I'm going to have to ask you to step out of the vehicle. You don't match the description of the escapee, but I'm going to have to give things a look-see."

Roy got out and was maneuvered by the trooper to face the SUV with his hands on the hood. The trooper carefully patted him down. Finding nothing of interest, he asked, "Can I search your vehicle?"

"Of course. Please be careful with the glassware in the back. We need it for tests."

The trooper clicked on his large flashlight and looked under seats, in the glove box, in the side panels and peered into all the boxes in the back. Again, nothing of interest to a non-Xylodonian.

"All right, Mr. Fed, everything looks hunky-dory. But I'm going to have to issue you a warning for not having that license though."

"Geez, thank you, officer. I sure don't need a ticket right now. Washington hasn't even set us our first paycheck yet."

"That figures," said the trooper, jotting on his flip pad. He tore off a piece of paper and handed it to Roy. "So, what's for dinner tonight?"

"What's for dinner?"

"You said you were going for takeout."

"Oh, yes. Yes, indeed. Chinese. I hope I remember everyone's order," said Roy. "Once you put it on rice, I guess it doesn't really matter, does it."

The trooper chuckled. "Probably not, sir. You have a good evening, now. Drive safely and don't pick up any hitchhikers."

"Thanks again, officer." The trooper waved him forward with his flashlight. Roy closed his eyes for a second in quiet thanks to his training officers. Then he smiled. *I didn't have to use my watch.*

The teams with the Security Corps spent their tours gathering data. Vast amounts of data. Some might call it surveillance; others might call it science. To Anton, Earth was one huge, living archaeological site. Most Xylodonian operatives avoided contact with humans unless absolutely necessary; that was protcol. Fortunately, Earth technology, at least in the advanced countries, made limited contact relatively easy. One could restock food supplies at self-checkouts or refuel vehicles in a similar fashion. Some supplies could be delivered conveniently via truck to one's doorstep. No communication with humans was needed. Heck, one could even buy lottery tickets from a machine.

Earth tours were easy duty because, by and large, humans tended to be stupid. For Xylodonian agents, the rules were simple—just obey whatever parochial laws exist, stay quiet, observe, report when required, then go home.

Anton was an exception. He liked mingling with humans, most of them anyway. Many humans, Anton observed, were like Welty's central character in "The Optimist's Daughter." Laurel McKelva Hand was at a cross-roads in her life, balancing an ailing father and a rival stepmother with her own past. She unearths fraught family secrets. Despite these peaks and valleys, Laurel puts her personal demons at bay and crafts a way to carry on. Most humans were much the same way, he had observed—nearly all human families had struggles and held secrets.

Ezra was one of the humans who Anton enjoyed interacting with the most. Anton met Ezra early in the first year of this tour. The "watches" (called holo-biometrometers) that Xylodonians were issued helped to maintain a human appearance, not difficult since the body structures were quite similar. In Anton's case, he assumed the guise of a fit thirty-five to forty-year-old Caucasian male with dark curly hair. The holo-biometrometers—at first glance, humans might speculate these devices were an invention of Q of James Bond fame—were the Xylodonian equivalent of the Swiss Army Knife. They had stealth and defensive capabilities, and since Xylodonian operatives couldn't just pop into Urgent Care, they had a variety of medical features as well.

One of the more common uses for holo-biometrometers—holos for short—was its "freeze" function to render opponents helpless. It was effective and non-lethal in keeping with Xylodonian law. The "freeze" had nothing to do with temperature; Xylodonian scientists had discovered that a light emission received through the target's optical nerve could suppress, even unravel, the motor skills functions within the brain. This light could be emitted as a beam or an array to vary the impact from individuals to groups. The planet's scientists had further refined the device to allow the user to permit some motor skills while inhibiting others. For example, a subject might be able to write their name while being otherwise incapacitated. Adjusting the wavelength also gave the user the ability to influence the compliance level of a targeted entity.

The training academy for Centurion Guardians had a language school, and Anton had excelled. Most Earth accents were easily mimicked; some, like the Gaelic variations, were to be avoided. Anton was able to shuffle through a variety of American dialects according to the situation. He was also fluent in twenty Earth languages.

Members of the observer teams from Xylodon were told to create and use human pseudonyms. Anton used the same name—Roy McDonald—in each of his tours. He had struggled to create a name until his first descent ten years before. As his vessel cruised over the New York State Thruway, he spotted one of those fast-food orgies at a prominent exit. There was a Roy Rogers restaurant next to something called McDonald's, which he would later learn is the garish child predator of fast-food restaurants. Roy McDonald. *Perfect*, thought Anton.

Anton/Roy had purchased a moped to travel about the Mississippi countryside. Hacking Earth currency was child's play for Xylodon; thus, purchasing food, clothing, and other supplies was never an issue.

It was a cool Sunday morning a year ago in March when Anton felt the desire for that Earth beverage he had come to admire—coffee. Like his fellow Centurion Guardians, he fancied it so much that he brought back different beans and blends after his first two tours.

He putt-putted down State Highway 304 toward Hernando,

## CHAPTER 2

which was near the junction of Interstates 55 and 69. Anton had learned that such locations often had overpriced dining and stale-smelling bathrooms to entice the bellies and bladders of travelers. One such spot was Waffle Barn.

Now, the café's namesake menu item, if covered with enough butter and maple syrup, was tolerable to Anton's tastes. He was not alone in thinking the greasy eggs and bacon might ski off the plate. The gravy for the too-hard biscuits was thin and tasteless. Hence, the sobriquet "Awful Barn." Anton had watched an Earth television program that starred an adventurous eater who, over two days, sampled everything on the Waffle Barn menu. Small wonder he's now dead, mused Anton.

But the Waffle Barn coffee was a different story. The coffee was spectacular, especially when compared to what Zephyra attempted to brew. And it came in sturdy, big-bottomed mugs, much like the waitresses who poured it.

Anton walked in and surveyed the dining room. Every stool at the bar was taken and every booth was filled. There was no waiting area, so Anton turned to try his luck elsewhere.

"Hey there, young feller. You by yourself? Looking for a seat?"

Anton pivoted and spied a white-haired man cast in an old man's standard uniform—a red-and-black flannel shirt and suspenders—beckoning him over. "This side of the booth is empty, and I could use the company," said the friendly diner.

Anton extended his hand. "Roy McDonald. Thanks for the seat."

"Ezra Hopkins. Some folks call me EZ. Most folks call me Gator."

"Gator? Now, there has to be a story behind that." A waitress—her nametag introduced her as Takeesha -- came over. "Just coffee," said Anton, now fully transitioned into his Roy persona. "Got time to share it?"

"Well, back in high school, Pudge McIlhany and me had gone out fishin' down by the creek over yonder. We came up on a gator sunning itself. Looked like he was sound asleep, so Pudge dared me to rassle him. In them days, a dare was serious business. Your manhood was on the line. Anyway, that gator was only about a five-footer, so I figured I could handle him. I snuck up on him, grabbed him around the middle and threw his lizard butt in the water. Everyone started calling me Gator after that."

"Great story. I love it," Roy said, taking a sip from his cup. "And you didn't get bit or cut up?"

"Nah, sir. Not a scratch," Ezra said. "Paul Bryant had his bear, and I had my gator."

Roy nodded and chuckled, pretending he understood the reference.

"I saw you pull up on that little scooter thang. Had to be chilly ridin' out there," Ezra said, adding a bit of sugar to his cup.

"Yes, but that's why God makes coats and hats," Roy replied. *I hope I named the right deity,* he thought. "Gets good mileage though."

"I bet it does. Where you from Roy? By your accent, you ain't from around these parts."

Roy gave Ezra his cover story. Was born and went to school up in the Northeast. Moved around because dad was in the military. Eventually got a degree in botany. Had been sent to Mississippi by the Department of Agriculture to study the flora and fauna of the South. No wife, no kids, no relatives to speak of.

"And what about you, Ezra?"

"Gator."

"OK, Gator."

"I have been around here all my life except when I was in the Navy fighting the Nips." (Anton didn't react; such regional colloquialisms had come to be expected.) "Got married after the war. Had four kids. The missus died about five years back, and the kids all decided to move to Florida or California. They have better things to do now. Different generation, different priorities."

"Sorry to hear that, Gator. Get lonely?"

"Oh, sometimes. But I gots my Waffle Barn, my Braves baseball, my Ole Miss football, and I still build a few bird houses."

"Bird houses?" The easy way "Roy" and Ezra had melted into conversation was one of the reasons Anton was comfortable with humans.

"Yeah, I was a carpenter by trade. A lot of the houses you see in Eudora and Hernando have my handiwork." Takeesha came over with fresh, steaming coffee mugs. Ezra's mug was different from Roy's.

The old man scowled. "Get-dammit, Takeesha. You know I only use fat-bottomed mugs. Like they had in the Navy. These here are only good for tea parties."

The waitress replaced Ezra's mug with one more to his liking. She winked at Roy on the process, a sign that the "mistake" might have been deliberate.

"That's better," said Ezra, taking a sip. "Coffee even tastes better in the right mug." Takeesha overheard him and laughed.

"So, what do you do in your spare time, Gator?" Roy asked.

"I builds the bird houses, and I got a young gal who paints 'em up and sells 'em on something called Betsy."

"You mean Etsy?"

"Yassir, that's it. Etsy. I don't know what it is, but it earns a few dollars for me and Ellie. She's my painter gal. It's coffee money anyway. Got to have my adult survival beverage," Ezra said, shoulders bouncing as laughed.

"On that, sir, you and I can heartily agree," said Roy.

"Hey, what time is it? I gots to meet up with Ellie," said Ezra, chomping a last slice of bacon and slamming back what remained of his coffee.

Roy pointed to his watch. "It's almost a quarter to eleven."

"Boy, I gots to run, or I'm a-gonna catch thirteen shades of hell from Ellie. That banshee's got a tongue that can fillet a river cat," said Ezra, wiping his mouth and standing. "But, Roy, I sure liked gabbing with you. I would love to hear more about the bugs and flowers you all are finding around here. And if you ever need a bird house, you know who to come to."

"It was a pure pleasure, Gator. Made my day."

"I'm here every Sunday and Wednesday morning as long as my back don't give out and my truck takes a charge. I'll save you a seat."

They shook hands. "That would be great. Count on it. It may not be every Sunday and Wednesday because some days are busier than others, but I'll try."

Ezra ambled toward the door as best as his creaking joints would allow. Takeesha looked over from the counter. "Ain't you hungry, sugah?" Roy/Anton raised his cup in surrender. "No, ma'am. Thanks though."

He sipped from his mug and watched as Ezra drove away in an old rusty, dirt-caked Ford pickup. *Yeah, no Nissans or Toyotas for Ezra,* thought Anton.

After throwing some cash under his mug, he walked out of the Waffle Barn, surprisingly warmed by more than the coffee. It was the first of many more meetings with Ezra and superior to any human-interaction instruction he had received on Xylodon.

It was one of those meetings that was the reason he missed his ride home.

# CHAPTER 3

*Somewhere near the rings of Saturn …*

"It's nice to be out of my Earth shape," said Zephrya, rousing from a space nap. Her unexpected pregnancy contributed to her growing moments of somnolence.

"My muscles get sore if I stay in these beds too long. Where are we?" she asked.

"A couple of hours away from Neptune Station," replied Termas. He had been manning the helm since takeoff. The Xylodonians had built Neptune Station, their closest facility to Earth in the Milky Way galaxy, almost two human decades ago. "We will need to get some supplies and refuel before we head home."

"Neptune Station? Don't you mean Base Buc-cee's? Or is it Buc-ees Station?" laughed Zephyra. She and Anton had so named the supply depot as such because it shared many of the features of its Earth counterpart—delectable snacks and spotless restrooms, at least so they had heard.

Termas harumphed. "You and Anton share too much of a liking for human culture and Earth amenities."

"It hurts not. Don't be the 'get-off-my-lawn' guy.'"

"Another Earth aphorism. *Girgach*! Is there no end to them?"

Zephrya enjoyed unleashing verbal volleys at Termas, but she had to be careful. He was easy to provoke, and their stealth departure from Earth had been stressful. Time to lower the temperature.

"Hey, do you remember when Jzargich-11 forgot to enact stealth mode over the Pacific and those U.S. Navy pilots chased him and filmed him? I have never seen a Xylodonian so embarrassed. Didn't he get suspended?"

"What a *nimnule*. Yes, I believe that was his punishment. Too bad; he was a good pilot," said Termas. The blowback led to a three-month pause in the Earth surveillance program. But the televised U.S. congressional hearings became somewhat of a hit comedy on Xylodon. It was at those hearings that the label for those mysterious aerial sightings transformed from *Unidentified Flying Objects* to *Unidentified Anomalous Phenomena*, a term that few Americans could pronounce much less understand. Perhaps that was the reason for the change.

Zephyra, now almost fully awake, had a more serious concern.

"What are we going to tell Sub-Protector Korphan about Anton? It will be rather obvious that something is amiss when only two of us get off the ship."

"We can tell him the truth. Anton disobeyed orders."

"But did he though? We don't actually know what happened to him. Stating that he did not follow a Protectorate command could lead to a nasty court martial. We would have to testify. And Anton does have his friends in the Protectorate."

"What did you have in mind?" Termas countered.

"We could just say that Anton volunteered to stay behind to be the lead prep for the next team. Or that he wanted to keep an eye on some important experiments. Or to make sure that our Earth samples didn't go bad."

"What about Anton? Wouldn't he tell the Protectorate a different story?"

"Not if we got to him first ... and told him why we were in a rush to leave," said Zephyra, rubbing a hand on her bulging lower stomach. "He would understand. I know it. He would agree that this one should be born on our home planet."

## CHAPTER 3

Termas put his arm around her. "Alright. I know some Guardians who might be able to get him a message. We can also figure out a way to make his silence worth his while."

"I feel so bad for him though. He's all alone in that horrid Mississippi place."

"It's only for a year or so. Anton will be just fine. He always is."

The two Guardians settled into their seats at the control panel. Neptune was now on the edge of the scanner.

Zephyra smiled. "Hey, I was just reading over our old preparation notes. Here's some trivia for you. Did you know that Buc-cee's was conjured in a place called Clute, Texas, by a human who went to Texas A&M University?"

"*Girgach!*" snarled Termas.

# CHAPTER 4

When debating whether Anton was being relegated to a life of perpetual loneliness, Termas and Zephyra had deliberately failed to include Jonnie Barnes Jr. in the equation. Barnes was the twenty-one-year-old son of the RV park manager. Not long after the Xylodonians had settled in, Barnes had dropped by with a six-pack of beer as a welcoming gift. It also allowed him to do some surveillance of his own, primarily of Rebecca, Zephyra's pseudonym. That visit, and others after, also allowed him to gauge whether there was anything to steal and pawn.

If one looked up "lowlife" in a dictionary, one might find Jonnie's picture as a representative example. Items around the RV park that were not locked up or chained down tended to go missing when Jonnie was around. Subsequent investigations by Jonnie's father, Jonnie Sr., could not determine the culprit. Some residents living in the park also complained to the manager about missing packages they were supposed to have received. Other residents complained about missing pets.

Jonnie never finished high school; he had spent many of those days outside liquor stores scamming for cheap beer and playing

# CHAPTER 4

"Ding Dong Ditch." That he and his gang of human excreta hadn't been shot in rural Mississippi was a minor miracle. He didn't have a defined job unless you call stealing catalytic converters a job. He was also prone to siphoning gas out of cars left overnight at auto repair shops as well. These were among his finer qualities.

He managed to make beer and cigarette money by being as skilled at putting on a front as the three "outsiders." He could be polite and would offer to run errands or tidy the grounds. The trio paid him to make meal runs or procure groceries and other supplies. Anton continued to utilize Jonnie occasionally after his two companions had departed.

"Where's Rebecca and the other guy?" Jonnie asked. Anton/Roy explained that they had temporarily been called back to Washington and that they might be gone for several months. There was disappointment in Jonnie's face.

It was no coincidence that Jonnie would appear suddenly at their RV when Rebecca was out in their backyard—what there was of it—catching some sun in her bikini. Once, she told Anton and Termas, she thought she caught Jonnie taking pictures of her with his cellphone. But she passed it off. *Humans are always taking pictures with their phones*, she rationalized. *Maybe that's just something they do.*

Jonnie rarely made conversation with Anton or Termas, but he wasn't shy about asking Rebecca if she needed any chores done or if she wanted to join him on the supply jaunts. There was something about his manner—and the fact that he seemed to be a stranger to a toothbrush -- that always made her respond that she was "too busy at the moment." That didn't stop Jonnie from trying to peek in Rebecca's window late at night when clouds shaded the moon. He was thwarted, however, by the RV's purposely darkened windows.

So, he found other windows instead.

# CHAPTER 5

Jonnie Barnes Jr. wasn't the only creature to have slithered out of Mississippi's sewers.

Terry Clyde Tolliver was practically engineered toward becoming a piece of human filth. He was on the conveyor belt of evil from the moment he emerged from his mother's belly. The fact that she died minutes later was a blessing; she never saw what she produced.

If human bile could be packed into a cookie cutter, it would look like Terry Clyde Tolliver. If a pustule could walk, it would look like Tolliver. Greasy-haired, blubbery and pimply behind thick-rimmed glasses, he had his own special franchise on mean. In the sixth grade he paid a couple of classmates a quarter each to give him a push in the back, which, ignorant of Tolliver's intentions, they agreeably did. Once shoved, Tolliver flew toward a nearby girl and placed his hands on her breasts to break his "fall." The girl slapped him across the face, but Terry Clyde didn't care. He had gained the desired inspiration for that evening's entertainment.

On another occasion, in art class, Terry Clyde snuck into the supply closet and urinated inside a fifty-pound bag of plaster of

## CHAPTER 5

Paris. His act wasn't discovered for several weeks, and although the teacher had her suspicions, there were no witnesses to verify them.

Terry Clyde, now eighteen, was an eighth-grade dropout. Technically, that was against the law, but the state of Mississippi didn't hunt for him too hard. He now spent his days watching internet porn and hunting squirrels with a slingshot. He and his sorrowful drunk of a father lived in the DeSoto County wilds, supported by dad's disability check from an oil rig accident.

Of late, he was staying up late posting personal lamentations on "in-cel" (involuntary celibate) websites and marketing his brand of hate on white supremacy sites, especially those that revered the Old South. These entities, with shared poisonous interests, welcomed Terry Clyde to their collective bosoms.

Terry Clyde had recently become enamored with Dylann Roof, the red-eyed, bowl-headed novice Neo-Nazi who killed nine Black parishioners at a church in Charleston, S.C., in 2015. Terry Clyde chortled over Roof's being able to sit in on a Bible study session at the church before pulling out a handgun. Roof had hoped to start a race war, even putting up a manifesto on a website called "The Last Rhodesian." Tolliver liked that. *Maybe I can be The Last Confederate*, he mused. He wondered about the thought process Roof used to select his target and what Roof felt as he viewed his handiwork afterward. The thought of being on the run, hunted by police, excited Terry Clyde.

He saw the mass shooting as a victory for the white race, noting that the police even bought Roof a Burger King meal after he was arrested. *I'd ask for a Jumbo Jack*, thought Tolliver. He also enjoyed the fact that President Barack Obama came to Charleston afterward for the memorial service. *I'd like the president to come see something I'd done. All the networks would be there, too.*

If Terry Clyde had any criticism of Roof, any flaw to be debated, it was Roof's choice of tools for his task. Oh, a .45-caliber Glock was a nice gun all right—for holding up liquor stores. But it lacked the magazine capacity and killing power of other items on the shelf. Handguns were a last resort, not a first choice for slaughter.

Tolliver got in his daddy's pickup—distinguished by the variety of NRA and "Come and Take It" stickers on the bumper and back window—and drove to the Walmart in Hernando. A plan was formulating in his muddled mush of a mind as he turned the truck radio to a headbanger channel. He went to the sporting goods section and stared lustily at the selections. A driplet of saliva oozed from the corner of his mouth.

"Gimme the AR-15. And some ammo. Got some wild hogs to get rid of," Terry Clyde told the clerk.

"Got ID?"

"Here you go."

The clerk looked at the card and then at Terry Clyde. He then took the card and went into a back room, emerging a few minutes later.

"Everything looks OK. How we payin' for this today?"

"Gonna need some ammo, too. Paying cash for everything." Terry Clyde had forged his father's signature on a check and withdrawn two thousand dollars. The clerk placed a half dozen boxes of ammunition on the counter.

"This do ya for now?"

"Uh-huh. Can you hold this stuff a minute for me? I'm a-gonna look around to see if there's anything else I need. Might need some camo for night huntin'."

Terry Clyde did indeed find a few items he hadn't thought of. They whittled away almost all his remaining cash.

He loaded everything into a cart and piled it into his daddy's truck. Took all of twenty minutes to put an instrument of death into absolutely the wrong hands.

## CHAPTER 6

You might say that Xylodon's interest in Earth took a serious turn the moment an American B-29 bomber flew over Hiroshima, Japan, on August 6, 1945. The Protectorate and government administrators in Xylos, the capital, had been aware of Earth's propensity for wars and other chaos and bloodshed for a century or more but had chosen to remain at arm's length. There were uninhabited planets that offered resources that were much easier to obtain. But the use of an atomic weapon against fellow humans sent shock waves through the Protectorate and Presidium, which had banned nuclear arms centuries ago. Planning for the Earth surveillance operation began almost immediately, resulting in numerous teams being dispatched across the unprincipled planet beginning in the 1950s.

Unforeseeably, the activity set off a reciprocal interest in possible space visitors by humans, some of whom continue to recognize World UFO Day. The "day" is set annually for July 2 to commemorate certain alleged events in Roswell, New Mexico.

Most Xylodonian teams were comprised of a trio of Centurion Guardians with a variety of skills. The Mississippi station was a new one, selected for its proximity to space exploration facilities, military bases, and a prime resource—water.

The days settled into monotony for Anton/Roy as fall arrived. Wake up. Dress. Coffee. Check the array data. Scooter over to various fields or woods—with owner permission to avoid being shot—to keep up appearances of being a botanist. He would peruse the occasional encrypted message traffic between the Earth surveillance teams and their handlers, most of it of the routine update and supply variety.

One alert did catch his eye—it was a reminder to report sightings or contacts with a Colorado-based Centurion Guardian who had not shown up for duty one day. Her team was given the important responsibility of monitoring the North American Aerospace Defense Command in Cheyenne Mountain, Colo. The Guardian's residence—they had rented separate apartments and an office for their "work"—showed no signs of violence, but a few pieces of Xylodonian equipment were missing. There were no clues as to her whereabouts. Her cover occupation was that of a teacher; when asked, the school administrators also had no idea where she was.

In the evening, Anton would eat something from a can or some of the Xylodonian staples left behind. Those were running low, though. He found himself enamored with the food channels on the television they'd bought.

"Why spend money on a television?" Termas, the most ardent penny pincher of the trio, had barked.

"Nearly all humans in America have televisions. Even if they don't have food, they have televisions. It would be suspicious *not* to have one," countered Anton.

Termas shook his head but gave in. That acquiescence eventually led to a bit of competition between Anton and Termas whenever a show called "Man Vs. Food" was broadcast. Termas, despite his niggardly manner, liked to gamble, and they would make bets on whether the program host would finish a five-pound plate of nachos or ten-pound platter of spaghetti.

Anton also liked the old westerns on the "Grit" channel, or any of the rampant British crime dramas. There mustn't be anyone left to

## CHAPTER 6

kill in Midsomer County, he and Zephyra would joke. Now, with Termas and Zephyra gone, he didn't have to battle over control of the remote. *That's one plus*, he thought.

The highlight of his newfound isolation became coffee time with Gator on Wednesdays and Sundays. Sometimes Ezra left before "Roy" got there because of a doctor's appointment or a "VA screw-up" or some other bother. He would leave a message with Takeesha to let Roy know. Neither Roy nor Ezra had cellphones—Roy, because there was no need; Ezra, because "fuck 'em."

On this September Sunday, as usual, Ezra was already at the Waffle Barn as Roy parked his scooter. Once inside, Ezra waved him over. Roy nodded at Takeesha, who grabbed a mug and brought it over.

"How you doing today, Gator?"

"Still vertical and ventilatin' for what that's worth," he said, smiling at his new friend.

Ezra and Anton had formed an almost professor-pupil bond, if not quite father-son. Anton as Roy could listen to the old man's tales of Depression-era Mississippi, chasing lightning bugs and putting pennies on train tracks, for hours. It was the reason he was late getting back to the ship. He didn't blame Ezra though. He blamed not being able to say goodbye.

"You're looking good, fella. Might want to get a new shirt sometime soon, though. That one looks like it's about done," cracked Roy.

"Baahhh. You and Ellie are just the same. Go pick another post to piss on. Drink your coffee, wiseass."

Roy laughed. Ezra was always good for expanding his regional human vernacular.

"No offense intended. Hey, last time we were here you said you would tell me some stories about your time in the Navy."

"I ain't forgot. I hate to bring it up. Just seems like most folks don't want to hear real history anymore. They'd rather let some pencil-dick on TV tell them what it is."

"Well, I'm not one of those. At least I hope I'm not," replied Roy, glancing with faux nervousness at his manhood.

"OK, then. You ever hear of torpedo juice?"

Roy shook his head in the negative.

"My brother, Zechariah ... Zeke, lord rest his soul ... used to make that stuff when he was on the USS Amberjack. That's a sub."

"During World War II?"

"Yep. Zekie and them old boys down in the torpedo room used to drain alcohol out of the torpedoes. They'd mix it with pineapple juice or whatever they had and have themselves a little cocktail party."

"Wouldn't they get in trouble?" asked Roy, recalling that such activity would lead to immediate dismissal from the Xylodonian Centurion Guardians.

"You betcha. If they ever got caught. Never did, but the Navy brass suspected something. They started putting all kinds of stuff in the alcohol fuel. One fella, Oklahoma kid, about went blind after drinking some of that crap."

"Wow. I'm surprised nobody died."

"There were rumors, but nothing was confirmed."

"So, when did you join the Navy, Gator? What ships were you on?"

"I signed up right after Pearl. I had never seen anything bigger'n Arkabutla Lake my entire life. Hell, I'd hardly ever been out of DeSoto County. But I wanted to be in the Navy."

Ezra turned his head to look out the window. "Zekie and I signed up together. I wasn't even seventeen. Lied about my age, and Daddy backed me up. Went through training, and they put me on the USS Bancroft in May of '42."

"What was the Bancroft?"

"A destroyer. New one. I was a kid, so I basically swabbed decks. Got to fire some AA guns a few times. Learned how the depth charges worked."

"See any action?" asked Roy, unaware of the delicate nature of such a question.

Ezra held up a hand and began counting off. "Let's see. First, we were up in the Aleutians. We rescued the Abner Read after it got its ass blown off by a Jap mine. After that, we did a lot of mischief from

# CHAPTER 6

Wake to Tarawa to Truk to Palau to Saipan. Then in late '44, I got transferred to a big boy."

"Big boy?"

"The battleship Missouri. You might have heard of it."

Roy pretended he had.

"Served on her till the end of the war. We sailed her into Tokyo Bay. I had a front-row seat to watch the Japs sign them surrender papers. There's a famous photo where you can see me sittin' up above 'em. I was tempted to spit, but I didn't."

"Amazing. You really did witness history."

"Yep. A bunch of kids making history. Lost a few of 'em along the way, though."

Takeesha came over to the table with a fresh pot and a third mug. Roy raised an eyebrow in surprise.

"Your girlfriend's here, Gator," announced Takeesha.

"Ain't got no girlfriend. The missus won't let me," Gator winked and then looked skyward in atonement.

Over to the table came a slim brunette in a t-shirt and paint-splattered overalls. Shoulder-length hair, blue eyes (not that Roy noticed). No makeup. Her dimples took center stage when she smiled at Ezra.

"Slide over Gator. You telling your stories again? Looks like you found another victim," she said, then looking at Roy. "Still can't say 'Japanese'?"

"Oh, hell to the no on that," said Ezra, giving the young woman some space on the bench. "Good mornin' there, sugar-puddin'. Roy, meet Ellie. Ellie, meet Roy. Now you're acquainted, and I can go back to my coffee."

"Ellen Atkinson. So, you're Roy. I've heard quite a bit about you," she said, hoisting her coffee mug in his direction.

"Good things, I hope. And I've heard about you. You do a little painting for our friend here."

"Yeah, he keeps me busy in my spare time. And it puts some coffee money in my pocket," said Ellie, giving Ezra a slight elbow jab.

"What do you do otherwise?" Roy inquired.

"I teach third grade at the elementary school in Hernando. It's like herding cats, but I enjoy it," Ellie said. "Gator says you are some kind of scientist."

"Botanist. And now you're going to tell me to 'leaf' you alone, aren't you."

"Ha. Good one. Bet you've used that line a few times. Get you anywhere?"

Roy wasn't sure how to answer Ellie's query. Then he remembered a line from the show "Wyatt Earp."

"Why, Miz Ellie. A gentleman doesn't say."

Ezra interjected. "OK, you two. Ellie, I got another bird house for you. The widder Thompson wants it. Says red and blue is fine for the colors. None of that psychedelic shit you like."

Ellie looked at Roy. "My, my, there are critics everywhere. Even hundred-year-old ones who can't see to drive."

"Ninety-seven," snapped Ezra. "See? Told you she had a mouth on her." Looking over at Ellie, he continued. "And I can see just fine. Hell, it's only nine miles between here and Eudora. I can do that in my sleep."

"A few times I think you did, looking at your truck," she said, glancing at Ezra and then back at Roy.

Roy played referee. "I'd say you two do know each other."

Ellie laughed. "He's all right for a potty-mouthed old sailor without a boat."

"Witch," said Ezra, who then winked at Roy. "Wasn't what I was gonna say. How come you ain't got no fella, Ellie? If you weren't so rattlesnake mean all the time you might get someone to hold your hand."

"Well, if there is anyone who knows what mean is, it's you. Besides, the guys around here just aren't my type. I need intellectual stimulation, which there's little of in the Waffle Barn," she countered before changing the subject. "So, what's my timetable on the widow's birdhouse, Gator? Do I have time to finish my coffee, or do I need to jump on this project right away?"

"That's up to you. The widder ain't gettin' any younger," Ezra said.

## CHAPTER 6

"You either," slammed Ellie, draining her mug."

"I set myself up for that, didn't I," said Ezra.

"Yep. Two points, Ellie," said Roy.

Ellie stood up to let Ezra slide out. She extended her hand to Roy. "It was a pleasure finally meeting you. Let's do it again some time."

Roy took her hand in a light grip. It was warm from the coffee mug, but soft. He found himself not wanting to let go.

"I'm glad to put a face with a name," Roy said. "I can't wait to see the finished product."

Ellie gave Roy an appraising look. There is something different about him, she thought. What is it?

"Well, I can give you my number if you need a guide around DeSoto County. Or protection from this old fool," she said.

"I'm afraid I don't have a phone at the moment," said Roy, then realizing that would sound somewhat suspicious to a thirty-something. "My contract is with the Department of Agriculture. Been waiting on the government to send me a phone. I'm just a poor botanist, don't you know."

"If you are waiting for the government, you may never get one," she countered.

"True. Tell you what. My headquarters slash casa is in the RV park just this side of Eudora. You can't miss which one is mine; it's the only one that looks like it belongs on Mars." The Anton side of Roy smiled at that one. "Drop in some time."

"I might just do that," she said. "C'mon, Gator, show me what you got."

Ezra smiled at Roy and winked, "Hell, you know I'm too old for that."

"Oh, my lord. You don't stop, do you?" she said, shaking her head.

"Two points, Gator. Game tied," Roy said.

"To be continued," Ellie retorted, taking Gator's arm and pulling him to the door. She looked at Roy. "Be safe in the berries and bugs."

"You do the same."

Anton watched as they went to Ezra's truck and as the old man fetched a bird house from inside the cab. No sound was needed, but he could tell Ezra was giving her instructions.

Suddenly, Anton thought, things have become more interesting in Mississippi.

## CHAPTER 7

Anton was under strict orders not to contact Xylodon directly from this station; there was a fear within Protectorate command that the signals would be detected by emerging Earth technologies. He would have to wait for an outside intermediary contact. His frustration grew with each passing day.

In the meantime, he kept up appearances of being a botanist. He traveled about the area seeking data on invasive plant species, of which there were quite a few in the state. Among these was the Japanese climbing fern (*Lygodium japonicum*), which had the nasty habit of covering trees and other vegetation, blocking vital sunlight and hindering photosynthesis. There was also the Japanese privet (*Ligustrum spp.*) and Japanese honeysuckle (*Lonicera japonica*), a dense shrub and an aggressive vine, that threatened to displace native flora.

I better not tell Ezra about those Japanese invaders, mused Anton, he'd be ranting for days. Much less say anything about the Chinese tallow tree.

Of course, there were other invasives species with less provocative names—water hyacinth and kudzu, for example. And Mississippi was home to one of the ten worst weeds in the world—

Cogongrass (*Imperata cylindrica*). That reedy little devil will outcompete native plants and disrupt entire ecosystems.

Anton's routine was to travel about and collect samples in the morning, and then write "reports" for the U.S. Department of Agriculture. These documents helped Anton maintain the ruse, but he noted that they were quite good. He sometimes wondered if he should provide them to local officials to help develop control measures and incorporate hardier alternatives. The interaction with humans and subsequent debate and scrutiny might be too much for his commanders, Anton decided.

He also began to dabble in studies on how climate change was impacting the state. Mississippi had already seen a two-degree Fahrenheit rise in temperatures since the early twentieth century and was projected to warm by an additional four to seven degrees by the end of the current century. In a domino effect, the state would likely see longer and more severe droughts. According to research Anton read, storms, particularly hurricanes, were likely to be more frequent and deadly, the latter impacting the entire Gulf Coast. A sea-level rise was another potential danger.

Anton was not the only Xylodonian observer to note how warming had impacted population migration patterns in Europe and the Americas, and the resulting immigration soups bore all sorts of consequences. He had seen evidence that some plant and animal species had moved northward to escape the warmer temps; others appeared to be declining from habitat loss. Each of these factors would likely combine to reduce crop yields and send the state's economy spiraling. Then there was the impact on human health—a link in his research had led Anton to data showing a steady rise in allergies and respiratory ailments.

Complicating the matter was the depth of human denial regarding the changing climate and its potential harm. Anton would often shake his head—the ostrich approach never worked, certainly not on Xylodon, where dogma's sway over logic had been kenneled long ago. Sadly, he thought, the overriding mantra in this corner of Earth appeared to be a preference for short-term gain over long-term pain.

# CHAPTER 7

It was mid-fall now. Anton/Roy had continued to meet and solve the world's problems—at least Ezra thought so—over coffee mugs with his human friend. Ellie sometimes joined them. Ezra noticed that Roy sat a bit straighter in his seat when Ellie showed up.

"You like her, don't you, Roy-o," Ezra tossed on the table.

"I do. She's funny. And I like listening to you both. You have given me a lot of history, but she gives me a lot of insights. She's very smart," Roy admitted.

"And pretty easy on the eyes," Ezra winked.

"I'm not going there. I'm a scientist."

"Sheeeeee-it. Yeah, you can try to hide behind that. You'll end up like me if you don't watch out."

Roy threw himself a conversation life preserver. "Hey, how's Ole Miss doing?"

"Pretty good. Only one loss so far. Reb coach has balls that clank when he walks. Goes for it on fourth down all the time. Usually makes it, though. Probably gonna bite him in the ass at the wrong time."

Roy/Anton wasn't sure what that meant, but he knew he'd steered the conversation away from dangerous waters.

On one bright and crisp October day, he had taken his scooter west on State Highway 304 to some empty stretches outside of Robinsonville. Casino money had provided some much-needed boosts to the state. Hernando, with its proximity to Interstate 55 had benefited. Eudora, on the other hand, hadn't seen as much as a trickle-down. But that locale and the surrounding vicinity was more appealing to a Xylodonian trying to maintain a cover. Anton would clip this and that, study it under a magnifier and put it in a plastic bag. Just what most folks would think a botanist would do. As he tromped about in his rubber boots, he had made a mental note to visit Arkabutla and Arkabutla Lake before it grew cold. He was curious about the water vegetation around there. Xylodon was a much drier planet, to which the inhabitants had adapted centuries ago. Still, the lack of water was an ongoing battle in some regions of the planet.

As the sun lost another battle with daylight-saving time, Anton returned to his scooter and put his "findings" in the backpack secured to the rear. He noticed the vehicle would get him back to Eudora but would need an overnight charge.

About twenty minutes later, Anton pulled into the RV park and parked the scooter outside what had become the center of his unexpected captivity. A piece of paper had been taped to the door.

"Dinner. Tomorrow night at seven. Be there. Casual. 1287 Beauvoir Drive. Ellie."

Anton gulped. "Uh-oh," he said.

## CHAPTER 8

Anton was not the only one spending time in the least populated areas of the county. Terry Clyde had found a secluded clearing in the backroads several miles off State Highway 301. It was a site that was reached after pavement turned to gravel then turned to dirt and offered perfect isolation. Tolliver had found it about two years back while cruising for a spot to smoke pot.

There was a rusted barrel near the center of a clearing where the road wilted into a dead end. The barrel had been used by someone to burn … what? Doesn't matter, Tolliver thought.

He took a two-by-six board out of the back of his truck and placed it atop the barrel. There were plenty of beer cans about, and he placed a half dozen or so of those on top of the board.

Tolliver then took the AR-15 out of the cab along with a two-liter soda bottle. Using some duct tape, he affixed the soda bottle to the muzzle of the AR-15 as a homemade silencer. It was a trick he had obtained from one of the supremacist sites he followed.

He counted off fifteen paces from the barrel (Terry Clyde figured that would be about right) and aimed. The .223/5.56 barrel was lighter than some versions of the weapon, but the smaller caliber round didn't produce the recoil of the heavier models. Terry Clyde wanted to judge the kick of the rifle and how fast he could return to his aiming point.

He knew the soda bottle could possibly misdirect some of the early rounds, but he wasn't concerned with that now. He wanted to muzzle the sound.

Pow. Pow. Pow. Pow. Pow.

Only one of Tolliver's shots missed the barrel or a beer can. "Good. Not too much kick."

He gathered some more cans and set those up. Tolliver then got another soda bottle and engineered a new "silencer." He removed the standard rifle stock and replaced it with a bump stock, allowing the weapon to mimic fully automatic mode.

Brrrrrrp. Brrrrrrrrp. Brrrrrrrp. Beer cans went flying; the barrel received a dozen perforations.

Terry Clyde paused to change magazines and grab a Bud out of the cooler on the front seat. He had about drained the first can when he spotted a scrawny tom cat passing through the far end of the clearing. Tolliver put down the can and quietly grabbed the AR-15, flipping the selector to single shot. Using the truck hood to steady his aim, Terry Clyde sighted the unsuspecting feline and pulled the trigger. The small animal was ripped apart.

"I think this will work," Tolliver judged.

# CHAPTER 9

Google Maps directed Anton to Ellie's residence in Hernando. He arrived just before seven and parked his scooter in the driveway behind her silver Tesla. He hadn't offered comment before regarding her choice of transportation, but he knew from what he'd read about his own vehicle that driving an EV could carry some political shade in certain locales.

Anton was torn about coming to Ellie's. It violated Xylodonian protocols on species interaction for one thing, and his gaps in knowledge of Earth cultures loomed as possible traps. But if he stood her up, that could weigh against him in Ezra's estimation, and Anton had no idea how long he would be stuck in this assignment. It was lonely enough as it was. Besides, Ellie seemed easy to talk to. Just eat some dinner, be polite, leave, Anton told himself. Ask questions, reveal nothing.

He grabbed two bottles of wine—a crisp Chablis and a bold cabernet—out of his scooter pack. He'd done some research on Earth customs that morning—bringing wine was something that dinner guests often did as a quid pro quo. Since he didn't know what was on the menu, he wanted to cover his bases, and the liquor store clerk helped him out.

He had to balance both bottles in his left arm to open the screen door and knock on the wooden front door. Music bellowed from within; it was Jon Bon Jovi's "Livin' on a Prayer," a lament about Tommy and Gina and their tumultuous life on the docks.

Anton knocked again, a bit more forcefully.

From inside the house, Anton could hear Gina making a second plea as to how she and Tommy could make it through life's tribulations if they could just stick together.

The music went silent. Padding feet approached and the door opened.

"Sorry if I didn't hear you at first. I'm a bit of a headbanger," Ellie said. "C'mon on in. Glad you could make it."

"Thank you for the invitation. Here's my contribution," he said, shifting to Roy mode and handing her the wine bottles.

"*Two* bottles of wine. Why, sir, do you mean to ply me with spirits and take advantage?"

Roy laughed (hoping that was the right response). "No, no, no. Your note gave me no clue as to what you were preparing. I wanted to cover all bases, as they say. Besides, I have no idea if you even like wine. If that's not the case, then feel free to pass these on to someone who will appreciate them."

"No problem. Wine is a survival beverage for third-grade teachers. We're just having spaghetti with meat sauce if that's OK. We can start with the red," said Ellie. "An Italian cabernet? You've done well, young man. Working for the government must pay well."

"Thanks, and not so much. I've never had this one, so I hope it's good."

Ellie was dressed in jeans and a light blue long-sleeved sweater. "Always good to get out of my school 'uniform'," she would say later. She led him to the kitchen and fetched two wine glasses from a cupboard. A large pot was bubbling on the stove. She put the Chablis in her fridge, opened a drawer and found a corkscrew. She handed it to Roy along with the cabernet. "You do the honors."

This could have been one of those awkward moments that Anton was worried about, but he had seen Zephyra open a bottle. This tool

# CHAPTER 9

was similar to the one she used, and he managed to remove the cork without any comedic moments. He poured two glasses.

"The noodles will be ready in a bit. We can sit and talk in here," she said, nodding toward a small den.

Roy sat in a cushy, leather chair—he deemed that a safe space. Ellie sat on the edge of a sofa nearest him, an end table between them.

"You like Bon Jovi?" she asked.

"Bon Jovi?" (*I haven't even sipped the wine, and I'm already trapped, thought Roy.*)

"That's who I was playing when you came up. C'mon now. You said you were from the Northeast. Jon Bon Jovi is a Jersey boy."

"Well, he's not the only one. Some of my friends thought he was too bubble-gum." (Sounded like a good answer.)

"Ha. You need new friends," she said. "He's a humanitarian, and we have similar politics. Did you know that he once performed on *Saturday Night Live* and then did a charity concert in Houston the next afternoon?"

Roy didn't know much about *SNL*, but he knew the distance between New York and Houston. "Wow. He must have slept on the plane."

"Probably. Some rich lawyer offered his charity a million-dollar check. He couldn't say no."

"What else do you listen to?"

"Pretty much anything from the eighties and nineties. The kids make fun of me. It's my daddy's fault. That is all he would listen to on his car radio, and it must have sunk in."

"What about today's music? R&B? Rap?" (Zephyra had talked to him about these human musical genres, although some examples didn't seem like music.)

"I will listen to Taylor Swift and Ed Sheeran and a few others just to prove to my students that I live in modern times," she said. "I better check on the noodles."

"Need any help?"

"Nope. Got it. Enjoy your wine."

After a few minutes of clattering and thumping, Ellie said, "It's ready. Come and get it."

Two plates of spaghetti slathered in meat sauce were on a two-chair table near a window off the kitchen. There were small bowls of salad and a slice of garlic bread for each of them. "There's parmesan, red pepper flakes, and salad dressing on the counter. Sorry, not much room on the table," she said.

Roy brought his wine over and sat down. He took a bite, noting he was being eyed for approval. "Very good. It's nice to get a hot meal for a change." Ellie smiled, then took her own bite.

As they ate, they chit-chatted about their daily routines—and not so routines. Roy told her about an encounter with a water moccasin that fell from a tree limb and almost landed in his rented canoe. She shared with him a case where one of her students was called to the vice principal's office for misbehavior.

"This kid was in training to become every 'mal' word in the book. The vice principal asked the boy what he wanted to be when he grew up. Know what he said?"

"What?" asked Roy.

"A serial killer."

"What? How does a third grader even know what that is?"

"I have no idea. TV, I suppose. There was that show about that Dexter guy," she said, sighing. "Just another thing education classes didn't prepare me for. And then there was the B-word incident."

"OK. Enlighten me."

"We were out at recess one day when one of my girls came up to me. She tells me that another of my students, Misty, had just called her the B-word. I went over to Misty and asked her if she called her classmate the B-word. She says, 'No, ma'am. Cunt doesn't begin with a B.' Yeah, she got a trip to the principal's office as well."

"Wow. Now I have to wonder what the first girl thought the B-word was," Roy said. "How did you up end with these kids?"

"Just lucky I guess."

They went back and forth on their personal histories, Roy sticking to his cover as best he could. Ellie talked about her educa-

## CHAPTER 9

tion classes and watching football at Southern Miss University in Hattiesburg and ticked off some of her early jobs. There was a second glass of wine for each and a second helping of spaghetti for Roy.

Ellie nibbled on her garlic bread. "Ezra said you had two folks helping you out until recently."

"Yes, they got called back. Now it's just me. But that's OK. I find I actually get a lot more work done without them around."

They talked about how much they enjoyed Ezra's stories, and Ellie related how she had met him for the first time. She had answered his ad in the weekly paper a few years back, and she had become painter-caretaker for him ever since.

He told her about the parts of the country he had explored. His voice quickened as he ticked off the types of plants he had collected.

Roy paused. "Oops, sorry. I keep forgetting that what's exciting to me can put other people to sleep."

"And that's the root of your problem," she said, winking.

Roy contemplated this slight jolt of surprise. *Oh, now I get it.* "I guess I will have to start branching out to stem the problem," he countered.

"Aaarrrgggghhh. I should have known better," said Ellie, "But it's nice getting some adult conversation for a change."

Then, after taking what Roy thought was a large swig of cabernet, she asked the next trap question. "So ... got a secret family back there where you're from? Leave broken hearts from New York to Boston?"

"No, I am one of those people who felt obligated to the people who funded my education," Roy replied. "And my overseers in Washington are really keeping me busy down here, so not much time for a social life. How about you?"

"I was married for a minute. Didn't work out. Got this house out of it, though," she said. "He took the dog."

"Sounds like a country song."

"Couple more glasses of this, and I'd be glad to tell you all about it. But I'll hold off for now."

Roy nodded an affirmation. "Here, let me help you with the dishes."

"Won't turn you down. I'll wash, you dry."

After getting things put away, Ellie offered him the leftovers. "I don't know if I can manage it on my scooter," Roy said.

"I insist," said Ellie, pulling out a Tupperware bowl and lid. "We can tape it down."

Roy started to protest, but thought: *No, dummy, this gives you a reason to come back.* "That's a great idea."

Ellie followed him as he put the plastic container into his scooter pack. "Oh, before you go. Let me show you where Ezra's slave does her work."

She opened the garage door—small wonder her car was in the driveway. The space was more artist's studio than garage. There were easels and work benches, and the walls bore at least twenty oil landscapes. There were watercolors as well.

"Wow, these are spectacular. You've been holding out," Roy said.

"Just a hobby."

"You should get them appraised. Seriously."

"Maybe someday," she said, then dropped the subject. "Say, have you ever been to Memphis? It's just up the road."

"No, but I've always wanted to go. I hear the barbecue is great."

"Alright then, we're going. Let me work out the details," she said. "You still don't have a cellphone? What about an email?"

Roy found a pen and scrap paper on a bench. He jotted down *Anton-7@gmail.com*.

Ellie squinched her face. "Anton?"

"That was the name of my first dog as a kid. Blame my parents. They were Francophiles."

"Ah, so cute. Well, let me do some research, and I will send you the details. I guess I will have to drive."

"It's a da- ... uh ... deal," said Roy. "Yeah, my little baby is only good for one. And you probably know the area better than I do anyway."

Roy walked with her to his scooter. Awkward moment number fifty-seven of the evening arrived. He looked at her and held out his

## CHAPTER 9

arms for a hug. "Thanks so much for this evening. It was great. You're cooking is much better than mine."

She squeezed back, then let go, taking his hand briefly. "Talk to you soon," she said, her hair wisping in the evening breeze.

He hopped onto his scooter and headed off. They exchanged waves as he departed. Ellie watched until he faded into the night.

# CHAPTER 10

Upon returning to Xylodon, Termas and Zephyra were allowed a day or so to recuperate from the long trip back from Earth. Their bodies had to readjust to their home planet, particularly the gravitational difference. Zephyra had no clue as to how that might affect her pregnancy. She did find that she could not stand on her feet for as long as she was able to on Earth. The drier climate also made her constantly thirsty.

She was napping when the order to report directly to Sub-Protector Korphan-2 was delivered by messenger. Typically, surveillance teams were required only to submit reports in writing and then provide details or clarifications in person if necessary. But this was an unusual circumstance.

A hovercar manned by Guardian recruits arrived at their domicile to escort the pair to Korphan's office in the main Protectorate building. Termas thought: *A hovercar? Escorts? To borrow an Earth phrase, we are in deep shit.*

Once inside the Protectorate, they were kept waiting for almost fifteen minutes outside Korphan's office. The escort remained. Finally, they were signaled in.

They stood at attention as Korphan, who had nearly sixty-five

## CHAPTER 10

years in the Protectorate, rose from behind his desk. He observed Zephyra's condition and gestured for her to sit.

He leaned on the front of his desk and folded his arms. "Before we get down to ... well, you know what, let me get the pleasantries out of the way. I trust you had an uneventful return flight?"

Termas stood rigidly, arms behind his back. "Yes, sir. Nothing unusual. Just the supply stop at Neptune Station."

"Good. Good. Anything unusual to report from your observation post in, what, Mississippi?"

"No, sir. I can't say we found anything appreciably different from the OPs in other parts of the southern United States."

"Well, we do have something unusual though, don't we?" said Korphan, glancing at Zephyra. "How are you feeling my dear?"

"Fine, sir," answered Zephyra. "Just tired all the time."

"How far along are you?"

"About eight months, sir." Xylodonian gestational periods were several weeks longer than those of humans; Zephyra had about two months to go before her delivery date.

"Congratulations, my dear. Not only for your child ... your first, right? ... but for setting Xylodonian history. This is the first time a surveillance team member has gotten pregnant," Korphan said.

"Thank you, sir," replied Termas.

Korphan looked up. "I didn't say I was pleased. This was not the sort of record I was looking for." Only in the last twenty-five years had the Protectorate allowed Guardians to couple, and only in the last decade had couples been allowed to serve off-planet together. Until now, no Guardian on off-planet duty had become with child.

"We don't have any regulations that cover this," Korphan said sternly. "But I would have thought two veteran officers would have better judgment."

Termas stammered, "Sir, I don't know what to say. I ... uh, I ... let me try to ..."

"Just be quiet. Are you going to explain to me why this happened? I *know* what happened, and I know *how* it happened."

"Yes, sir."

Korphan shuffled through some papers on his desk and held up a document. "As I said there are no protocols for this situation, so there are no prescribed punishments. Suffice it to say, however, you two are confined to Xylodon duty for the foreseeable future."

Termas and Zephyra nodded. "Understood," they said in unison.

"Now, tell me about Anton. Why was he left behind?"

Termas had decided to abandon his original cover story, fearing it was a devil's brew for him, Zephyra, and Anton. Not knowing the full truth, he had decided to track it as best he could.

"Sir, because of the Earth's orbital position at the time and because of commercial flight schedules, we only had a small window for departure," Termas said, looking toward the ceiling as if it held his rehearsed statement.

"Go on."

"Anton was off on a data-gathering mission. He liked to go alone."

"It helped him think, he would always say," Zephyra interjected.

"It wasn't the first time he was late getting back to the OP. But he was told what time he needed to be back for star-tether," said Termas, glancing at Zephyra. "He knew it was important."

"Any idea if he was injured? Or worse?" asked Korphan.

"No, sir. We couldn't make contact," Termas replied. "If I can be frank, sir, Anton would often leave his communicator behind."

"Why? That's not procedure."

Zephyra explained: "Anton was stopped once while driving his two-wheeled vehicle by a human law enforcement officer."

"It's also not procedure to break subject planet laws."

"He didn't," Zephyra said. "But that doesn't seem to matter in Mississippi. Anyway, the human searched Anton's vehicle and found the communicator. Anton was able to explain it to the human's satisfaction. But after that, Anton was nervous about bringing it with him."

Korphan smiled. "Anton was always a quick-witted fellow. Made him perfect for the teams."

"Yes, he's a survivor. We all know it," said Termas. "He has shelter, he has food, he has Earth resources and, as you said, he has his wits. He's the best of us."

## CHAPTER 10

"That he is. Hence my concern." Korphan walked about the room for a moment, then approached a large bookshelf. He fingered a volume or two, then turned.

"All right. This is what we will do. By 'we', I mean me and not you two. You've done enough," said Korphan, pleased with his little joke. "We will send a scout ship into Earth orbit to make contact with Anton. But it will take time to arrange a crew and even longer to put together and transport a new surveillance team."

Termas came to attention. "Sir, I would like to vol…"

Korphan cut him off. "Don't even ask. You have other matters to attend to. I'm putting you in charge of writing the new pregnancy protocols for our regulation manual. Got it?"

"Yes, sir."

"What about me, sir?" asked Zephyra.

"Well, you aren't going anywhere anytime soon, now, are you?" Korphan said. "Motherhood is your only mission for the time being. Then we'll see."

He returned to his desk seat, shaking his head as he looked at Termas and Zephyra. "Dismissed."

## CHAPTER 11

Anton/Roy and Ellie set their Memphis plans for the first Saturday in November. Ellie kept most of the details to herself, instructing Roy to rendezvous at her home around 9 a.m. He had told Ezra about the Memphis trip during their regular Wednesday get-together, and Gator just smiled—one might say in a proud way—and said, "You kids have fun."

On Saturday, Roy scootered over—wearing a leather bomber-style jacket to ward off the chill—and knocked on her door.

Ellie emerged wearing a white long-sleeved shirt, denim jacket, jean mini skirt with a frayed hem and dark brown cowboy boots.

"Don't you look nice. But aren't you going to be cold?" Roy asked.

"No worries, plant man. We won't be outdoors that much today," she said. "Hop in my silver beast and we can get going. We can stop and get coffees along the way."

Memphis was barely a thirty-minute drive from Hernando once you got on the freeway. But there was a noticeable difference. The closer one got to the state line, the landscape appeared more … modern.

They made small talk over their coffees as Roy tried as best he

## CHAPTER 11

could not to stare at Ellie's tawny, slender legs under the steering wheel. He told her about his latest vegetative findings; she told him about how her students were gearing up for Thanksgiving. "Even the serial killer?" he asked. "Even the serial killer," she said, laughing.

Roy looked at his newly acquired cellphone, partly to get caught up and partly to take his mind off Ellie's legs. He flipped through a few stories on his social media until he had to eye-brake on one. He chortled and shook his head.

"What's so funny?" Ellie asked.

"You have to hear this. Don't be fooled by the beginning of the story. It's told by a guy whose father died."

"Oh, that's always a hoot."

"Hold on. You have to listen to the whole story."

"OK, go for it."

Roy read from his phone:

*A man went to a Dublin cemetery to visit his deceased father, making a stop at a florist shop to find a remembrance to place on the gravesite. As the father was a beloved figure, the man returned each week to the cemetery, bringing new flowers with him each time. Other family members had done the same, removing the old bouquets and creating quite a floral display each week.*

*After several months, the man again came to the cemetery to pay his respects. This time, he couldn't help but notice the shabby condition of the grave next to that of his father. Thinking back, he couldn't recall seeing a single flower left on that grave, whose headstone read simply "Warren McTavish. 1942—2003." On his next visit to his father, the man pulled a flower from his purchased bouquet and left it on McTavish's grave. He also pulled some weeds and tidied up the site as best he could. The man repeated the gesture the next week and the week after that.*

*Eventually the man became curious about why no one attended the grave, so he conducted some research into Warren McTavish. It turned out McTavish had come home one night, murdered his wife, then murdered her aged parents and killed their dog. He then went to a nearby railway station and threw himself in front of a train. The lurid truth explained why McTavish had never received flowers. Knowing that he had been placing flowers at the grave of a killer shocked and embarrassed the man. He had to find a way to make amends.*

*He did some more research and learned where McTavish's wife and her parents were buried. As he had done before, he purchased some flowers and brought them to the wife's cemetery, dividing the flowers equally between the three graves. He stood back and began to pray. As he finished, a woman approached him. "I've never seen you before," she said. "Why are you leaving flowers on my aunt's grave?"*

*The man sheepishly recounted what had led him here and expressing dismay that his gesture of kindness could have been misconstrued. The woman told him that she was impressed by his generous, although misdirected, concern for someone he had never met. The man asked her, "Would you like to get a drink at the pub?" She said yes.*

*A year later, he asked her another question. She said yes to that one as well.*

"And that is how I met my wife."

Roy chuckled again. Ellie responded with, "Oh, my God. OH, MY GOD. What a great story. There's a lesson in there, you know."

"Indeed," Roy winked and said, "Flowers are the way to a woman's heart, even when they aren't for her."

"That's not the lesson I had in mind, but you are probably right," Ellie said.

About ten miles from the state line, they noticed a filmy haze settling onto the roadway. A panoply of brake lights heralded the unexpected slowdown. A familiar smell told them that the haze wasn't fog, it was smoke. As Ellie crept forward, she spotted the source of the delay.

"Looks like a grassfire. People are always flicking their cigarettes into the grass, which is pretty dry this time of year. Dry grass plus lit ciggies equal grassfires."

Roy looked at Ellie. "Well, you know what the firemen will say once they get here, don't you?"

"No ... what?"

"Look ... Mississippi Burning," he deadpanned.

Ellie shook her head. "My God. Get out. Get out of this car right now."

## CHAPTER 11

They both laughed as the procession began to gain speed. Ellie thought to herself: *He's smart, decent looking, and he has a sense of humor. Where did this one come from?*

After they crossed into Tennessee, Roy queried, "What's first up on the agenda?" He had done some pre-trip research so he would not appear suspiciously unknowledgeable about the city's history and top tourist offerings. But he had no idea what Ellie had in mind.

"Part of this is going to be driving tour. But we'll stop at a few places that I think you will enjoy," she replied. "And, yes, you will get your barbecue."

"You are a queen among women," Roy said.

She stayed on I-55 until it branched to Riverside Drive, allowing Roy a brief glimpse of the Mississippi River and the assorted shipping accoutrements. She then went right on Union Avenue to Danny Thomas Boulevard.

"Danny Thomas was a comedian on a show called 'Make Room for Daddy' back before we were born," Ellie said. (*Well, before you were born,* thought Anton.) "He founded a children's hospital that's now known worldwide. We'll be coming up on it a minute."

"Yes. St. Jude's. That's the facility that handles kid cancer patients, right?"

"Yep. And they don't charge the families anything."

St. Jude's Research Hospital was indeed founded by Danny Thomas—who was fulfilling a vow to his patron saint—and some friends in 1962. Its patients are under age twenty-one, with some exceptions, and must be suffering a catastrophic ailment. Cancer was the primary villain. The hospital, supported by around two billion dollars in donations annually, sees about 8,600 patients a year. There are seventy-seven beds for patients requiring hospitalization during treatment. The campus also has housing facilities for patients and their families. Thomas' daughter, Marlo, a comedic actress, is the national outreach director for the facility.

Roy had memorized that information but didn't say anything. He felt that oversharing information might be suspicious as well. Or make him appear nerdier than he wanted to.

Ellie turned into the campus and drove around the facilities. Roy was struck by the emblem of a praying child affixed to several buildings. "They do a lot of good for the world here," Roy said.

"Several years back, one of my students suddenly dropped out of class," Ellie said. "I found out she was being treated here. I guess they got to her in time because last I heard she's still with us."

Roy nodded his head. They both were quiet until she pulled back onto Danny Thomas Boulevard.

"OK. Time for something a bit more upbeat," she said. Guiding the Tesla on a few zigs and zags, Ellie was soon on Elvis Presley Boulevard. Roy knew immediately where they were headed.

"The home of The King," he said. "It this a drive-by or are we going in?"

"Going in."

"Since you are doing the driving, I insist I pay for the tickets."

"I can pay my ..."

"No arguments."

Ellie gave him a slight frown, but said, "OK, then."

Roy smiled and changed voices. "Well, bless-a my soul."

"Woo hoo, you go hound dog."

They opted for a self-guided tour and sauntered through the interior of the colonial mansion. Oddly, despite being the home of the King of Rock 'n' Roll, being inside seemed to usher visitors into a church-like demeanor. Using the headphones as a guide, they went from room to room, viewing recording areas, Elvis costumes, and the walls filled with platinum and gold records. They toured the grounds and auto museum, then ended by honoring the memorial resting place of the rock star and his family. Before leaving the area, they trekked over to see Presley's two private aircraft—the Hound Dog II and the smaller Lisa Marie.

"My mother was madly in love with Elvis," said Ellie. "If I had been a boy, I would probably be named Elvis."

"You would have been great on the 'Ed Sullivan Show' I bet," Roy said. "You hungry yet?"

"Indeed, sir. Next stop: Beale Street and the Blues City Café."

After a few minutes, large red letters announced that they had arrived at their destination. They didn't have to wait long for a table.

# CHAPTER 11

Roy held Ellie's chair. "My, ain't you a gent. Thank you, sir," she said.

Roy looked over the menu. "This is fantastic. Can I get one of everything?" he asked.

"Suit yourself, but this time I'm paying, so be gentle." Ellie's expression indicated personal harm could be forthcoming for any protest.

Roy started with some Memphis soul stew then moved on to some ribs. Ellie ordered a catfish plate. Iced tea for both.

They returned to the Tesla. Ellie noticed a drop of barbecue sauce on Roy's jacket. She moistened a tissue with her the tip of her tongue and wiped off the sauce.

"There now. All better," she said.

"Man, I need a nap," Roy countered.

"Not yet. A few things else to see."

The Tesla's GPS successfully guided them to the National Civil Rights Museum.

"Isn't this where Dr. King was killed?" asked Roy, referring to the 1968 murder of the famed civil rights leader. "The Lorraine Motel?"

"Yes. The museum incorporates the motel. You'll see," she said.

This time they went Dutch on the tickets. The museum was an eye-opening experience for Anton. It was a testament to overcoming hate, a hate that has not dissolved but evolved. It was a hate that had become the currency of political expedience. Xylodon did not have the diversity of Earth; perhaps that is why such hate had never taken root there.

Ellie and Roy passed the North Carolina lunch counter exhibit and stood in the Rosa Parks bus. They read quietly about the Little Rock Nine and the Philadelphia (Miss.) Three. Roy gritted his teeth, but Ellie was glad to see children touring the museum. "They don't let us teach about this in school now," Ellie said.

"Why not?"

She leaned toward him and whispered, "The children and the grandchildren of the massas might get their little feelings hurt. Can't have that. It's OK to blow up little girls in an Alabama church, but don't tell little Johnny and Joanie about it."

Roy closed his eyes and shook his head. Yet another subject where logic didn't apply.

"Here's some trivia for you. Ole Miss isn't just the name of that college in Oxford. Back in the slavery days, the 'ole miss' was the senior female house slave. The university decided a few years back to avoid using the term on its official correspondence. You would have thought it was the end of the world."

"Wow. How do you know all this?" asked Roy, mentally noting how diversity was appreciated on his planet.

"I read," said Ellie.

At the end of the tour, they came to the exhibit of the room where MLK spent his last night. They saw the bloodstain on the concrete walkway. For Roy, it emanated pain and anger and despair even after five decades.

It was almost dark when they left the museum. Ellie could see that Roy was holding on to some emotion. They got in the Tesla and began to head back, back in time. "One more thing to see," she said. "We won't stop though. We are running out of daylight."

Ellie hopped onto State Highway 14 to Ford Road and then Honduras Avenue. She stopped in front of Otis Redding Park.

"Otis Redding?" posited Roy.

Ellie looked surprised. "C'mon now. No way you haven't heard of him."

Anton realized it was a trap moment, and he was in it.

Ellie hummed, then sang about sitting in the morning sun.

Roy suddenly remembered the song. He joined in, finishing up with a high-pitched rejoinder on wasting time.

"Oh, *that* Otis Redding. Forgive me. Temporary brainfart," Roy said.

"I forgive you. He was born in Georgia, but he did a lot of recording in Memphis. So, Memphis adopted him," Ellie said. "Yet another artist who died in a plane crash."

"Probably better than dying on your toilet," Roy said.

"You have a point. Anyway, too late to go in. There are walking trails and other stuff to see and do. Some other time maybe. Just wanted you to see it."

## CHAPTER 12

Ellie hit the gas and before long they were back on I-55 and headed to Hernando. The trip home was a recounting of what they had seen and consumed. But at one point Roy remembered something Ezra had said when he first met Ellie at the Waffle Barn. Roy reached up with his left hand and took Ellie's right in his.

She looked at him and smiled. *I get the feeling there's something he's not telling me,* she thought. *But until he does, this can work. This can work just fine.*

The Tesla was soon in its resting spot, and Ellie hooked up the charging cable. Roy told her, "Thank you so much for today. This was the best day I've had since … since I don't know when."

"Well, let's cap it off with a glass of that Chablis you brought over. I haven't opened it," she said.

His Anton side was hesitant. The Roy side said go with it.

He went with it.

They entered, and Ellie took their jackets and tossed them on the den chair Roy had sat in last time. It was hard to mistake the home for being anyone else but Ellie's. There were Atkinson touches all about. The whole interior felt … what's the word? … welcoming.

Ellie went to the fridge, grabbed the Chablis and handed it to Roy. "You know the routine," she said, retrieving two wine glasses.

They sat on the sofa at a respectable distance. Ellie untucked her shirt and took off her cowboy boots to reveal little pink footlets. Roy glanced at the whiteness of her legs, then quickly turned his attention to his glass.

Ellie caught him looking. "Hey, you. I'm over here," she said.

"Sorry. Just thinking."

"About what?"

"About what we saw today, and what one can learn from it. I guess it's the scientist in me."

"So, what did you learn?"

Roy paused, collecting his thoughts. A misstatement could be dangerous for him.

"Well, death is strong. Death is powerful. Even the rich, the powerful, and the angelic cannot escape it. But amidst death and desperation, there is hope. And hope, while it doesn't always win, is often the strongest runner in the race. How'd I do, teacher?"

Ellie looked at him; her mouth opened. "Those were some amazing insights. I truly had no underlying intentions for going to any of those places. I just thought you would appreciate them."

"Something else I learned."

"What's that?"

"Memphis ribs are damn good."

Ellie laughed. Then she set down her glass, got up and walked over to Roy. "You know what else is good?" she asked. Anton froze; Roy was curious.

"No, but I think you are about to show me."

She took his glass and sat it down. She straddled his lap and put her hands behind his head and leaned in her head to put her lips on his. Tongues intertwined. She kissed his cheeks, chin, neck then moved back to his lips.

Roy pulled back from the embrace. "There's something I have to tell you. I am not very experienced at this sort of thing."

"Shhhh," said Ellie, putting a finger to his lips. "I'm a teacher." And they joined lips once again.

## CHAPTER 12

Roy kept his hands to his side at first, but then instinct took over. He moved his hands to her hips, then to her sides and back. Her scent was intoxicating. She offered no resistance as his hands moved to her breasts, first on the outside of her shirt and then underneath. He opened her shirt, pushed up her bra and began kissing each proffered porcelain mound.

Ellie suddenly stood up. She reached under her denim skirt and removed a pair of white cotton panties. She unbuckled Roy's belt and pulled down his pants. Then she straddled him again, grasping the back of the sofa. His hands slid up her legs to her buttocks.

They became joined once more. And again. And again. And again.

## CHAPTER 13

In the morning, Roy awoke spent. That was more physical activity than he had experienced in this entire mission. A floral scent pervaded the bedroom, quite the pleasant change from the smell of stale sweat in his RV. He turned toward Ellie's side of the bed, but she wasn't there. Before he could get up to investigate, footsteps approached.

"Good timing," she said, handing him a mug of coffee. She was dressed only in his shirt, which provided minimal modesty. It reminded Anton of an episode of "Sex in the City" he had watched with Zephyra as part of her "research." One of the female characters wore her partner's garments on the "morning after." That was supposed to mean something, Zephyra said, but Anton couldn't remember what it was.

"Good morning. Thanks," Roy said.

"And good morning to you." She gave him a kiss. "It's amazing what you find when you get old McDonald off his farm."

"Ouch. Too early. And I'm not old." They both laughed.

She nestled in next to him. Roy raised the mug. "Aren't you having any?"

## CHAPTER 13

"It's Sunday. I thought I would wait until 'The Gator Story Hour' for my coffee."

Roy shot up. "That's right. Gator. What time is it?"

"Don't worry. We have time. Ready for another lesson?" said Ellie, reaching under the covers. Roy put down the mug. "Yes, ma'am."

An hour or so later, Ellie and Roy arrived at Waffle Barn; she in her Tesla and he on his scooter. They used separate vehicles to maintain a degree of pretense for Gator, who they could spy watching them from his favorite window booth.

They walked in and sat down, but this time Ellie sat next to Roy instead of Ezra.

"Good morning, Gator," they said, almost in unison.

Ezra looked at Roy, who was looking at Ellie. Then he looked at Ellie, who was looking at Roy. Then a laugh welled up from deep within him.

"Well, now," he said, grinning. "How was Memphis?"

## CHAPTER 14

Over the next few weeks, Anton spent most of his evenings at Ellie's. He had even purchased a cheap cellphone; only one number necessary. He would usually show up after her needed decompression time and would stay unless she was overwhelmed by schoolwork. That was the case one night, and he felt like an intruder. Sometimes he would bring dinner over. His first attempt at cooking would have earned a novice rating, but Ellie gave a polite evaluation. It didn't matter—dessert was always better.

Ellie brought him in one day for a "show and tell" session with her students. A room of third graders can be a rowdy herd, but Roy riveted them with his comparison examples of leaves and grasses from the Northeast and Mississippi.

"Who likes to play in the dirt?" he asked the class.

"ME. ME. ME. ME. ME," the kids shouted, waving their arms in the air.

"That's good, because we can learn many lessons from things that grow in the dirt," he said to begin his demonstration, which included a simplified explanation of photosynthesis. At the end, he told the children, "So from now on when you get dirty, just tell your parents you were doing science experiments for Ms. Atkinson."

## CHAPTER 14

Ellie took over. "Let's give Mr. McDonald a big hand, class." As the students cheered, she turned to Roy and whispered, "I'll thank you later, hot shot. But I've got some people I want you to meet before you go if you have time."

"My time is your time, Ms. Atkinson."

Ellie led Roy to the teacher's lounge, where the noontime gaggle had gathered. Four women were animatedly chatting over salads and iced tea. "Roy, this is the gang. Gang, this is Roy. Roy McDonald. He was the dog-and-pony show in my class today. From left to right we have Kendall Guthrie, Sofia Hernandez, Janis Li, and Wendy Cosgrove. Kendall is the school secretary, and these others pretend to be teachers."

"So, this is the famous Roy," said Kendall, wiping a bit of ranch dressing from the corner of her mouth.

Roy looked at Ellie. Her eyes were upturned to the ceiling. "Oh, boy," she said under her breath. "Here we go."

The verbal fencing began. "Famous, eh? Just how famous am I?"

"I hear you are some kind of bigshot plant expert," said Kendall.

"Well, yes, I do my best to get to the root of their problems."

Kendall let loose with a laugh that appeared to emanate from the bowels of the battleship Missouri. Her three companions dropped their forks and laughed—at her. Roy noticed that Kendall's iced tea was a bit more diluted than her companion's drinks.

"Unless, of course, there is mathematics involved. In that case it becomes a square root problem."

Kendall's cackle eruption caused the lounge door to shake on its hinges. She put a hand to her chest and bent over to collect whatever oxygen was passing by. When she rose again, she fanned her face with both hands.

Ellie just shook her head. "Roy, you've found an audience."

Kendall breathed deeply, then said, "Looks like you got a good one, Ellie."

Before Ellie could reply, Roy jumped in with, "I hope she won't be branching out anytime soon."

Kendall put her hand over her mouth. Janis then gave Roy "the look," in a jesting (half jesting?) manner. "Roy, you can come to my class any time you want."

Roy's face reddened. Ellie made a cat noise, then said, "OK, it's time for him to go. He has leaves to collect."

"Pleasure to meet you all," Roy said, turning for the door.

"You better be good to our Ellie, or we'll come hunt you down," Kendall said.

That conjured up an image of being chased by four women armed with salad forks in Roy's mind.

"Well, we can't have that, can we? Besides, I work for the government. We're here to help," he said as Ellie grabbed his arm and led him away.

"Thanks again for coming by today. The kids loved you. I'll get the reviews from the gang in a few minutes I'm sure," Ellie said. "Watch out for that Kendall though. She's always up in my business. She thinks my life is her life."

"Thanks for the warning," he said. Roy leaned in to kiss Ellie, but she raised a finger to her lips. "Not in school." A long hug became the school substitute.

Days past as days do. Anton's time with Ellie was easy and comfortable, like that old pair of shoes one grabs without reflection or regret to run a quick errand. She introduced him to seafood gumbo, jalapeno cheese grits, craft bars, and big hair bands. On Saturday, they went to some nearby casinos. With the help of his watch—it did much more than maintain his human appearance—Ellie was able to win $105 on the slot machines. "Wow … almost matches my teacher salary," she said. Roy "lost" twenty dollars.

On the nights he stayed at the RV, Anton would spend the evening reading or completing the fake reports needed for his cover. It was on one of those occasions that he was alerted to an incoming message.

Anton went to his computer station and called up the message. It was encrypted, a clue that it was a communication from the Protectorate. He ran a decryption subroutine on the message and read:

## CHAPTER 14

*"We are making arrangements for your recovery. Be aware there are some complications on our end. Further instructions will be forthcoming.*

*Stay strong, Guardian.*

*Sub-Protector Korphan*

*Forthcoming.* I wonder what that means, Anton thought. A few months ago, this would have been a welcome message. Now, Anton was not as certain.

## CHAPTER 15

A day later, Roy was bent over his desk reading some intriguing articles from *Scientific American* and *Technology*. He already had stored the digital version of the two articles, but now he was furiously highlighting what he had distilled to be their quintessence. One of the articles outlined testing in Abu Dhabi of the Atmosphere Zapper, a device that used electricity to pull rain from the atmosphere. Parts of Xylodon were not far unlike Abu Dhabi, Roy noted. The theory involved sending negatively charged particles into the air to smash kamikaze-like into super-cooled droplets and turn them into precipitation. *Would the atmospheric differences be too much?* he wondered.

Xylodon's water scarcity was not as dire as, say, Singapore on Earth. Yes, Xylodon used real-time data to monitor and manage water flow, just as Singapore—an island city-state—did. Water consumption was highly regulated on Xylodon, but it had still more than doubled in the last decade as the population increased. In comparison, water use in Singapore had increased twelve times since it had obtained independence from Malaysia in 1965. How Singapore oversaw its water difficulties—most of its water was imported

# CHAPTER 15

from its former parent, Malaysia—was why Xylodon had embedded a surveillance team there.

The other article was also of high interest. As on Earth, cloud-seeding held some promise; Xylodonian scientists were hoping to see at least the 10 percent to 15 percent increase in rainfall expected by human scientists under the right conditions. The peculiar meteorological conditions and unpredictable wind patterns had made cloud-seeding a less advantageous option, a hurdle that Xylodonian technology, for all its wonderful achievements, had not yet been able to overcome. It was a vexing question—if Xylodonians could transform matter, why couldn't they make it rain?

The second article was even more intriguing. Another group of human scientists and engineers, again in Abu Dhabi, were attempting to use nanotechnology to stimulate and expedite the condensation process. *Why hadn't we thought of that*, Roy wondered. Xylodon was no stranger to nanotechnology but using it for cloud-seeding had not been considered. These revelations might be the impetus for putting a surveillance team in the United Arab Emirates, he thought. He would need to forward this information post haste.

But not at this moment. Roy jumped in his chair from the hard KNOCK-KNOCK-KNOCK at his door. He opened the door and was pleasantly surprised by the radiant presence of one Ellen Atkinson. Her silver Tesla was gleaming in the parking lot; he hadn't heard a vehicle pull up. She was wearing a red-and-white checkered blouse and "painted on" jeans right out of the Billy Ocean song. Her ears were adorned with large silver hoops. There appeared to be a splash of makeup, but she didn't need it.

"Well, hello there. Wow. My day just got better," Roy said.

"C'mon. You're done. It's almost five. It's quitting time even for Yankee botanists," she replied.

"If you insist. I know better than to argue with the toughest third-grade teacher at Hernando Elementary. Come in a minute while I freshen up."

Ellie stepped into the RV and looked around. "This place could use a woman's touch," she said, running her finger through some windowsill dust.

"No doubt. It could use a man's touch, too, but I've been pretty busy during the day. And there's some Hernando hussy who keeps me distracted at night. Housecleaning has had to wait."

"Hussy?!?! Why, sir, I'll have you know I haven't been a hussy since ... since at least high school," Ellie said, hands on hips. "Now quit stalling. Go get ready."

"Where we going?"

"You up for a movie? We haven't done that yet. I hear that it's standard procedure for dating couples."

Roy blinked at the word "couples," but he replied, "That sounds great." He turned toward a back room and closed the privacy door. After taking off his shirt (tossed on a bed), he went into the bathroom. He quickly washed under his armpits and slapped what pretended to be cologne on his face. A replacement shirt was found, along with a light jacket just in case.

"Ta daaaa. All ready," he announced, popping out of the back room.

"What's all this?" Ellie asked, nodding toward the magazines on Roy's desk.

"Just a little light reading for us science types. There are some remarkable ideas out there for increasing precipitation. Mississippi gets plenty of rain, of course, but not every place is Mississippi." His home planet's capital of Xylos, with its often-rigid water-use regulations, came to mind.

"And don't we all thank the good Lord for that," she said. "OK, let's get on the road."

After they got in her Tesla, Ellie's nose began to twitch. "What is that you have on?"

"The shirt?"

"No, that smell."

"Too much? I'm the first to admit that my sense of smell is not that refined."

"I've smelled worse. OK, something else for the list."

Roy started to inquire about this list but was slightly worried about what else might be on it. Instead, they chitted and chatted about how their perspective days had played out.

## CHAPTER 15

"Where are we headed and what are we going to see?" Roy asked.

"I really wanted to take you to the Ritz Theater on Commerce Street," she said. "It was one of those old-fashioned movie theaters with the huge marquee out front. But it closed down awhile back, and then it got bought. But the new owner turned it into a food market or something like that."

"Interesting. We ought to go check it out some time."

"Maybe so. But tonight, we are headed to the DeSoto Cinema Grill. It has 'Oppenheimer' still playing. Are you up for that? I figure the buzz has worn off by now, and we should be able to get seats without a problem."

"Sounds good to me. It has a great cast."

After a few minutes, Ellie whipped into the cinema parking lot and found a space with a charging station. "Who says Mississippi is backward?" she winked at Roy. "By the way, the movie tickets are on me. You can get dessert afterward."

Roy couldn't resist. "Now I have to pay for dessert?" he said in his lewdest voice.

The retort earned him an elbow in the ribs. "Not that dessert. Real dessert-dessert, you dummy."

Roy chuckled and Ellie just shook her head as they entered the rope line for the ticket booth. They were up next for tickets when Roy noticed a black pickup truck cruising slowly past the theater. The truck's tinted windows allowed only a silhouette view of the driver. As the truck went past, the familiar black cannon-emblazoned "Come and Take It" stickers could be seen on the back. Then the truck was out of sight.

"That was odd," Roy said. "Can a truck give you the heebie jeebies?"

"I had the same feeling," Ellie said. "C'mon, let's go." Then to the ticket clerk, "Two adults for 'Oppenheimer,' please."

They stopped for sodas and a large popcorn to share before heading to their recliner seats. One of the ads shown during the previews had Marlo Thomas extolling the virtues of St. Jude's Hospital. "I wish we'd had more time to look around there. Seems like they do a lot of good," Roy whispered. Ellie nodded her head in agreement. For the Anton side of Roy, the ad planted a seed.

The popcorn was gone after the first hour or so of the three-hour film. At that point, Ellie's hand slipped into his for the duration.

Afterward, Ellie drove to a locally owned ice cream shop. A couple of waffle cones—hers with chocolate mint; his with butter pecan—were soon dripping in their hands as they took a table.

"What did you think of the movie?" she asked between licks.

"Cillian Murphy was fantastic. He seemed to personify the moral dilemma in creating such a weapon."

"There's no dilemma for me," Ellie replied. "It was terrible. The first atomic bomb was dropped on Hiroshima in August 1945 and killed around 140,000 people. It was dropped by a B-29 flown by Col. Paul Tibbets that was called Enola Gay. You know what Enola Gay is backwards?"

"No idea."

"It's a backward anagram of sorts for 'You and God alone.' Enola Gay was also the name of the pilot's mother."

"You said the bomb was terrible. But didn't it bring about the end of World War II? Prevent the Allies from having to invade Japan?"

"Maybe. They had to drop another bomb on Nagasaki first, and that killed about 75,000 more people," Ellie replied. "Couldn't they have tried more diplomacy before blowing up more kids?"

"Possibly. History is not likely to tell us," Roy said. "I can see you have some deep feelings on the subject, and I respect that. But you should respect those who might feel another way about it. I think our friend Ezra would fall into that group." As he offered this defense, he knew Xylodon had long had nuclear and even deadlier weapons but had honored treaties to never use them on the planet unless necessary or by agreement.

"You mean Mr. I-will-never-buy-a-Japanese-car? Yes, you are probably right," she said. "Doesn't make me wrong, though."

Roy munched down what remained of his cone, then looked up to see the same black pickup he had noted at the theater driving past the ice cream shop. Again, the driver wasn't visible, and again the

## CHAPTER 15

same stickers came into view as the truck went past. This time, Ellie noticed the truck, a four-wheeled malevolence, as well.

"You about done? I think it's time to get out of here," Roy whispered.

"I'm with you. Let's go."

As they stood beside Ellie's Tesla, they watched the pickup and its cargo of foreboding leave the parking lot.

# CHAPTER 16

Sub-Protector Korphan looked out at the red-orange landscape of Xylodon from his tenth-floor office window in Xylos, the planet's capital city. It was a dry planet, almost arid in some regions. The planet had seas and lakes, but nothing like the massive oceans on Earth. Here, there was barely enough water to support a population half the size of Earth's. The problem was a meteorological one: not enough rain. That was why the far more aqueous Earth was deemed such a enticing curiosity. Its atmosphere created ample rain, almost too much in some cases. Xylodonian researchers hoped to replicate that atmosphere, but more data was a constant need. Korphan was hardly alone among Xylodonians who were contemptuous of how humans treated their planet. *You wouldn't find islands of plastic waste floating in our waters,* he often sneered.

But he had to admit that the vegetative samples brought back from Earth were of high interest. Some specimens appeared to hold water in dry climates and could be highly beneficial. Many had failed to take root unless in a controlled environment. A popular plant grown indoors was something called a tomato. It was quite tasty and could be consumed with a variety of food items.

Members of the Protectorate had their concerns, however. Earth

## CHAPTER 16

was a violent planet. Its denizens seemed to prefer spilled blood to attempting compromise. Division and hate peppered human history. Animus toward the "other" was a constant—whether it be race, class, religion, gender, or political philosophy. And, in what caused ongoing consternation for Xylodonian observers, humans never seemed to learn from their own history. Thus, the research missions were also sheathed in constant surveillance of human advances.

There was something else worrying the sub-protector. It was the proverbial itch he could not scratch. When he had served as a young Guardian, there were at least two occasions when a surveillance scout had gone "native" on hospitable planets. One had been found and prosecuted; the other had blended into the stew too well. Now, he was dealing with two "itches" on Earth—a missing Guardian and the tardy Anton.

Korphan was sipping a cup of Colombian coffee, a human concoction that was considered a delicacy on Xylodon. One of the Guardian surveillance teams stationed in Earth's Southern Hemisphere had brought it back when its tour concluded. Just the aroma itself seemed recuperative. The sub-protector considered himself somewhat of an Earth coffee connoisseur; he could talk at length about the merits of café au lait versus chicory. He considered brew cups to be an abomination and was hoping that someday he could sample a strange-sounding human brew that was fashioned from coffee cherries passed through the intestinal system of a feline. Supposedly, entering the smaller life form into the brewing equation reduced any acidity.

The communicator on Korphan's desk hum-buzzed to life. He clicked and replied, "This is Korphan."

"Sir, this is Trajanus-8 in Transport Section."

"Yes, go ahead."

"Sir, we have a craft ready for the recovery mission you requested."

"Excellent. When can I expect star-tether?"

"We still need to update the ship's stealth devices."

"I thought you said it was ready."

"The propulsion, guidance, communications, and defense

systems are ready. The stealth system is just an upgrade to the latest version all our ships are using. It shouldn't take long, sir. Probably the end of this week."

"Thank you for the update, Trajanus. Let me know the moment the updates are completed."

"Yes, sir." The communicator went silent.

*Now to find the right crew*, Korphan said to himself.

## CHAPTER 17

Ellie was relaxing on her sofa, a highlighter in her mouth and her feet in Roy's lap. He was massaging them, patiently awaiting his promised evening with "Forrest Gump." Ellie was reading an education magazine. She would occasionally grunt, highlight furiously, then return the highlighter to her clenched teeth.

Suddenly she sat up. "I've never read so much crap in my life. Science of Reading, my ass," she said.

Roy knew to play along with Ellie's tirades, but this one had him curious. "Science of Reading?"

"There's this woman podcaster who makes herself out to be a journalist. Only she ain't no more a journalist than Yogi Bear." Anger tended to bring out the Mississippi in Ellie's vernacular, Roy had observed. He had only a vague idea Yogi Bear was, but he knew it couldn't be good.

"Journalists are supposed to give both sides of a story, right? Only she gives just one side—hers—and lies about the rest. She cites studies that aren't real studies."

"Give me an example of what her 'side' is," Roy said.

"She thinks that phonics is the solution to every type of reading problem kids have. When you only have a hammer then every problem is a nail. Let me tell you one thing I learned at Southern Miss, knowing how to make a sound or pronounce a word does very little on its own for reading comprehension."

"I was never taught phonics," Roy said, truthfully.

"Pronunciation is great, but it only goes so far," she said. "Take the word CREEK. In most places it's 'creek' with a long E sound. But some folks pronounce it crick. Well, 'crick' can be like a pain in the neck. So, pronunciation does nothing to promote understanding. You can teach a kid to say 'bub-ble,' but that won't teach them how it was created or why it floats."

Roy thought, *Wow, she's on a roll. Do I stop her or let the train run through?* He nodded in agreement. "Once again you are being too logical," he said. "But you look great up there on that soapbox. Continue."

"I did studies on child reading development. Trust me, being able to mimic a sound does little to help a kid with dyslexia. I've had kids with dyslexia. They often need a reading specialist to help them navigate their reading until they are able to do it well on their own. The feds provide money for that, but a lot of districts don't want parents to know that. But that's a whole 'nother story," she said. "Suffice to say there ain't no science in the Science of Reading. It's a sham."

"Have any journalists … real journalists … done stories on this?"

"A few, but there's others who don't dig far enough," she said. "There's a lot of big money on the podcaster lady's side. And I do mean *big money*. They get a school district to buy into Science of Reading, and then they pop up with all sorts of materials to sell to the district. Like I said, big money."

"How do you—and those who agree with you—fight back when the other side has all this big money?"

She paused and thought. "I'm not sure. It's a PR battle against disinformation. And this is one where the disinformation side is winning. Just like those book-banning bastards in Florida and Texas. Moms For Liberty, my ass. Liberty for them, censorship for the rest of us. Menopause can't come fast enough for those crones," she said. "One of the books they like going after is *A Handmaid's Tale* by

## CHAPTER 17

Margaret Atwood. I think they want to ban it because it actually lays out their game plan for society going forward."

Then the Ellie train jumped onto a different track. "You know about the Establishment Clause, right? Separation of church and state? Basically, the Founding Fathers of this great land forbade the establishment of a national religion. They also protected the practice of any religion," she said. "Now, a whole lot of groups have sprung up that are trying to tear down the wall between church and government. They all have names like 'Patriot this' or 'American that' so that the seem wrapped in the flag. You have school board members in public schools advocating this mess. They want to bring religion back into schools, just as long as it's the right religion, of course. Muslims, Jews, Buddhists, or atheists need not apply."

Roy wanted to say this would never be an issue on Xylodon but that was a subject he had to steer miles around.

"I'm sorry, Ellie. I know all of this has to be frustrating to you. Seems like a lot of folks prefer the simple answer to the more complex one. There seems to be a lot more heat than illumination these days," he said. He gave her leg an empathetic rub. "How's about some popcorn and Tom Hanks to make you feel better?"

She slapped the magazine down. "Run, Forrest, run."

# CHAPTER 18

The dawn oozed from the Earth's womb in a pinkish glow on Wednesday, December 13. "It's D-Day," said Terry Clyde Tolliver.

He was dressed entirely in black, including his heavy boots and beanie cap that could transform into a balaclava mask. He put on a tactical vest that had pockets for six additional magazines of .223-caliber, 62-grain rounds. There was a full clip already in the AR-15.

Terry Clyde placed a gym bag carrying other items he thought he might need—his father's six-shooter, a hunting knife, pepper spray, bandages, cellphone—on the passenger floorboard of his pickup. He got in the cab and placed the AR-15 over his lap. He had filled up the truck and checked the tire pressures the day before. The weather was overcast but otherwise clear.

*Nothing to hold me back*, thought Tolliver. Just one more thing to tend to first.

He took the old revolver and went back into the house. A few minutes later, he was back in his truck cab.

"Goodbye, dad. Have a good day," he said, putting the truck in reverse.

The black-clad teen had scouted his intended target over several

## CHAPTER 18

days. Terry Clyde knew that the first recess period at the Hernando elementary school was around 10 a.m. The school was bounded by streets on four sides, but Pondberry Street had fewer trees and an almost unobstructed view of the playground.

Tolliver drove away around 9:15 a.m., giving himself plenty of time to hit Highway 301 then take 304 to slink into Hernando. He drove at or just under the posted speed limit. "Don't want to be pulled over today," he told himself. "I'm gonna be on CNN."

Once entering Hernando, he turned onto Goodman Road. He drove past Renasant Bank and Buck's Bargain Center and a raft of other small businesses. He paid no heed to the holiday discounts advertised; his attention was affixed elsewhere. He turned briefly onto Commerce Street and then slowly entered the residential area with its clean sidewalks and driveway basketball hoops. Terry Clyde recalled something he had read once: The lawns are well-manicured. *Where did "well-manicured" even come from?* he wondered. *Did they use fingernail clippers on the grass?* It may have been the only original thought that Tolliver ever had.

He turned onto Pondberry. The neighborhood was asleep. "It'll be lively soon enough," Tolliver said to himself. He pulled his truck to the side and stopped. It was 9:38 a.m.

---

Inside the school, Ellie Atkinson was having a bear of a day. She was trying to educate her twenty-two students on how to count syllables but with little success. With less than two weeks to go before Christmas, she was losing the competition to skateboards, video games, and Barbies. The kids knew that Christmas break was coming in two days and there was a party in store.

The class was filled with so much humming and whispering and shuffling, that Ellie just gave up. "All right. All right. All right. We will go outside in just a minute."

"YAAAAAAAAAY!!!!!!" came the collective class response.

"But first: Have you all finished your Santa letters?"

"YES, MS. ATKINSON!"

"Everybody? You sure?"

"YES, MS. ATKINSON."

"OK, then. Get your coats because it's chilly outside. Then form a line in the hall."

Even with the playground just twenty steps aways, the students were still overly frisky. Ellie had to stop two boys who were pinching one another. She moved to the front of the line and gave the command to advance. After a few steps, she looked over her shoulder. Like little penguins, she thought.

She held open the exterior door, and the children burst onto the playground like a shaken soda bottle. Some headed for the swings, some dashed to the slide, and others gathered in their usual groups to plot the day's mischief. Ellie stood toward the center, playing ringmaster.

---

Tolliver surveyed the playground; the kids were scattered everywhere. That was something he couldn't predict. *So, how to do the most damage in the least amount of time*, he thought.

He pulled forward about six feet, giving him a optimal view of the playground's central area. Tolliver placed the truck in park but kept the motor running. He then leaned over and rolled down the passenger window until just a few inches of glass were visible. He leaned back and rested the AR-15 muzzle on the top of the window. A bit too low, so he reached over and adjusted the height, paying no attention to the yelps and squeals coming from the schoolyard.

He pulled down the mask, flipped off the safety on the AR-15 and resighted the rifle. He placed his right forefinger on the trigger.

---

Hernando police officer Bobby Gene Holloway turned his patrol car onto Pondberry and looked at the controlled chaos going on outside the school. Just in time, he thought. Holloway had just returned to his

## CHAPTER 18

usual shift after two weeks on nights. He loved this morning shift, especially being able to time his school drive-by with the likely appearance of one Ellen Atkinson. She often wore tight sweater tops, and on warm days when she wore a skirt, a friendly breeze would cooperate with some interesting views. He and Ellie had gone out a couple of times—for coffee and bowling—but nothing romantic had emerged, at least not from her end. She ended whatever was between them without explanation. She was cool, but not chilly, so on occasion he would stop at the school, approach the playground fence and the two would chat.

There she is. Lucky me, thought Holloway.

He was hoping to stop today, but he noticed a pickup truck in his usual parking spot. The blue smoke from the truck's muffler indicated the truck's motor was running. There was no license plate on the front. The tinted windshield concealed the driver. "Now, ain't that odd," he said.

---

Terry Clyde had begun to increase the pressure on the trigger when he noticed movement to his left. A police car had settled in about 15 feet away from the front of his pickup. Shit, he thought, what do I do? He lowered the AR-15 from view.

The police officer got out of his vehicle.

Shit. Shit. Shit, thought Tolliver. He let go of the rifle and put the truck in drive. He eased to the left, then drove away, not looking at the cop.

---

Holloway started to jump back in his cruiser and pursue the pickup, but at that moment he heard: "Hey, Bobby Gene. Merry Christmas." It was a smiling Ellie Atkinson.

Holloway looked at the fading pickup, then back at Ellie. "Hi, Ellie. Merry Christmas, yourself. I see you've lost control of your Indians."

"Never fails, especially this time of year. I haven't seen you in a while. Not been sick, have you?"

"No, it was my turn to do nights for a couple of weeks. Not seeing you was the worst part."

"Bless your heart, you sweet talker, you."

Holloway approached the school fence. "Hey, Ellie. I was wondering if you might want to go out and do something sometime."

"That's very nice of you to ask, Bobby Gene," she said. "But I have to be honest with you. I've been seeing someone for the past few months, and things are going pretty well."

"Damn. Oops, sorry. Hope the kids didn't hear," said Holloway. "Well, he's a lucky fella. ... I assume it's a fella."

Ellie laughed. "Yes, he's a fella."

"Well, if something changes, the offer still stands," said Holloway, moving back to his patrol car.

"Thanks. You're sweet," said Ellie. A school bell signaled the end of recess.

Holloway got behind the wheel and started to pull away.

"Just my fucking luck," he said to himself.

---

"Just my fucking luck," Tolliver said to himself. *I was going to be famous. I was going to be on the cover of all the newspapers.*

Terry Clyde continued to look in the rearview mirrors to see if the cop was tailing him. So far, he was in the clear.

There will be other days, he told himself as he turned onto 304. Patience is a virtue and all that.

Tolliver, driving carefully, looked over to roll up the passenger window. He'd forgotten it until now. As he rolled up the window, he saw the Waffle Barn. A large black woman was pouring coffee for some old man in a red flannel shirt.

*Well, well, well. That'll do,* he thought.

He looked ahead and then in the rearview mirror. Tolliver slowed, pulled partly onto the shoulder and negotiated a U-turn. He

## CHAPTER 18

then pulled into the Waffle Barn parking lot and stopped parallel to the building. He got out of the cab, AR-15 in hand, and went behind the truck bed. The black woman was still visible talking to the old man. He leveled the weapon at the glass window.

---

Anton/Roy was a few minutes late for his regular Wednesday coffee congress with Ezra. I'm going to catch hell today, he thought.

As his scooter neared the restaurant, Anton noticed a pickup parked in an odd way. Even odder was the man dressed all in black behind the truck.

---

Terry Clyde let loose a laugh born in Hades as he unleashed a volley into the restaurant, going from one window to the next, loosely aiming at torsos and heads. Glass shattered. Dishes flew. People screamed.

---

Anton could barely process the horror occurring before him. *No. No. No,* he thought. He jumped off his scooter and let it fall. He moved toward the shooter.

---

Now Tolliver spotted a figure at the end of the parking lot moving toward him. He hit the magazine release and grabbed a fresh one from his vest and slammed it home. Terry Clyde turned toward Anton.

Anton looked him in the eyes. Perhaps it was Anton's expression that caused the shooter to pause. Or perhaps the shooter thought Anton was unarmed and he had more time. In any case, in that moment Anton touched his watch.

---

Terry Clyde tried to pull the trigger, but his finger wouldn't work. He tried again with the same result. Tolliver tried to take a step but still he found himself frozen. He looked at the man in the parking lot. He was still touching his watch.

It was then that Terry Clyde Tolliver, unable to control his limbs, put the AR-15 muzzle into his mouth and blew his own head clean off.

## CHAPTER 19

It was cold and raining on the day of Ezra's funeral. It always seemed to rain at funerals. The damp seeped into the black suit and overcoat Ellie had helped him pick out. Ellie soon had to remove her black heels after they bit into the muddy terrain.

Dozens of people had gathered to mourn the death of the unofficial mayor of Eudora. Roy examined the crowd. What part of Ezra did they share with him? The salty Navy veteran? The carpenter? The bodacious storyteller? The reptile wrestler who earned the name Gator? Or the kind and generous soul who would offer a seat to a stranger?

Ezra Tompkins was one of six people whose lives were extinguished at Waffle Barn on December 13. The other victims included Takeesha, an assistant manager, and a family of three that included a four-year-old girl. They died quickly but horribly from an object with one purpose—killing quickly and horribly. Police later found the body of Tolliver's father inside his home. He likely never felt the bullet that killed him.

The service for Ezra was quite moving, Roy thought, although the religious references cast by the minister seemed ill-fitting for the occasion. The series of Gator stories told by longtime friends were more to his liking. There were a few distant relatives, including Ezra's children, who received the prime seating. It was believed to be their first visit to DeSoto County in decades. Most who knew Ezra at the end said Ellie and Roy were more family than those out-of-towners.

Ellie held tightly onto his arm when they entered the cemetery. He could feel her shudder with grief. She couldn't bear to watch as Ezra was lowered into the ground. Roy had never encountered human grief before, and he was a bit stunned when it enveloped him as well. He still saw a smiling bewhiskered face with steam from a coffee cup rising before it, mischief playing in his eyes. As each clump of dirt hit Ezra's coffin, Roy felt a chapter closing.

Roy was later surprised to learn that Ezra had written a will; Gator usually had little value for such things ("Feeding the vultures," he called it). Roy was even more surprised to learn that Ezra had left him his Navy ribbons and commendations. Ezra also decreed that any bird houses or other of his woodshop items would go to Ellie.

After the services, they drove back to Ellie's house in silence that felt like a mourning shroud. The shock of the killings lingered heavily on them and the county as well.

Roy and Ellie sat on her sofa, and she glanced at her Christmas tree. She gave a sharp moan, like that of a wounded animal, and collapsed in tears once again.

Under the tree was her gift to Ezra—a fully painted bird house.

## CHAPTER 20

The days after the shootings and funerals poured forth as if by rote, or like the script of the world's most tragic play set on repeat cycle. After all, as Anton read in news accounts, the United States had witnessed more than six hundred mass shootings already during the current year, and nearly forty of those saw four or more deaths—which raised it from being a "mass shooting" to "mass killing."

Anton asked in shocked wonder: Did humans really have to create definitional pockets for levels of repeated outrage? He remembered an Earth scientist had once proffered a definition of "madness." That seemed to fit here.

As for "here," the scene played out much like the six hundred or so before it.

Mounds of flowers, wreaths, and signs were placed outside the Waffle Barn as makeshift testaments to the tragedy. Some folks left toy gators as a remembrance to Ezra. Pictures of Takeesha and the other victims were also placed. As for the Waffle Barn itself, it never recovered from its wounds.

The sound trucks and cameras of state and national news media descended quickly upon the quiet county like ravenous wolves.

DeSoto County couldn't house them all, so reporters encamped in Jackson or along Interstate 55. Terry Clyde Tolliver would have been furious to learn that CNN and other news outlets would not only not use his picture, but they also wouldn't use his name either. But there were always some that did.

Politicians rolled out the usual statements about "thoughts and prayers for the victims"—as if they had the slightest clue about who the victims were, as if thoughts and prayers could stop a bullet. Some politicians demanded "action on gun control now"—but they never took it.

The police investigation went quickly—it was more of a cleanup than an investigation. The perpetrator was dead. Through officer Bobby Gene Holloway it was revealed that the Waffle Barn had not been Tolliver's initial target. Many postulated aloud and on social media that if Holloway had acted when he encountered Terry Clyde then the tragedy could have been avoided. His chief defended him, but the pressure grew to be too much for Bobby Gene, and he eventually resigned. Another victim.

The primetime news shows again turned to their selected pull-out experts to give context and meaning or just fill airtime. But they could never answer the why, why, why or assuage the pain.

A few days later, the next mass shooting came. It was a synagogue in Pennsylvania; twelve elderly worshippers—half of them Holocaust survivors—were shot to death. And just like that, the Waffle Barn was forgotten.

# CHAPTER 21

One enigma from the Waffle Barn massacre remained: Who was the mystery man who seemed to confront Terry Clyde Tolliver in the parking lot? The survivors didn't get a good look at him, and the man didn't stick around. There was no security camera footage to assist.

Save for visiting Ellie, Anton went as underground as possible. He paused his visits to the DeSoto County countryside and hid his scooter behind the RV lest some witness remembered seeing it. His trips to Ellie's house were well after dusk, shielding his identity.

The Earth holidays came and went almost joylessly for Roy and Ellie, still weighted down by their grief for Ezra. A few days before Christmas, Ellie handed Roy a piece of paper.

"Take a look at this," she said. "That's one of the Santa letters I got from one of my students."

Roy gazed at the scrawled handwriting.

*Dear Santa,*

*Please don't bring me toys this year. I only have one wish. When you drive your sleigh this year, please bring an extra big sack. And after you deliver presents, please put all of the guns in your sack and take them to the North Pole. If you do that then maybe the people will stop crying.*

*Thank you!*

*Bobby Whitburn*

Roy shook his head and looked at Ellie. "Why is it that children get it, and adults don't?"

There were peaks, however. On Christmas Day, they sprawled on the floor and took turns opening the packages under Ellie's small yule tree. Her first package concealed a variety of woolen scarves. She cooed delight as she tried on all four of them. Roy opened a package that held a gift card to be used toward a better cellphone.

Ellie then ripped open a midsize box and removed the padding therein. She found LP records for the bands U2, Def Leppard, Poison, Metallica, and Guns 'N Roses. She gave Roy a hug, and said, "Now I will have to invest in a turntable. OK, your turn."

Roy tore the wrapping paper off a leatherbound volume of "The Drunken Botanist: The Plants That Create the World's Great Drinks" by someone named Amy Stewart. "Oh, wow," he said as he flipped through the pages. He looked at Ellie. "I see what you're doing here. You want your own personal botanical bartender."

"Yeah, I guess you could say that's a gift for the both of us," she said. Ellie opened her final gift from Roy and discovered a rather expensive bottle of Chanel perfume. "Oh, thank you, thank you, thank you. I could never afford this in college. She opened the container and put some perfume on her wrist, then rubbed her wrists together. She then held a wrist to Roy's nose.

Roy's eyes widened. "WOW. That is amazing. You'd better not wear that to class, Ms. Atkinson. Those third-grade boys might go wild."

"Oh, hush. Don't even put that out in the universe. Besides, those hellions are wild enough as it is," she said. "There's one more box for you under there. It's kind of small, so you might have to search for it."

Roy leaned over on all fours. When he did, Ellie hand-smacked

## CHAPTER 21

him on his rump. He turned his head. "I had a feeling that was coming."

He retrieved the gift Ellie had placed near the back and opened it up, revealing a match box. He slid it open.

Roy held up a shiny key and gave Ellie a puzzled look.

"Welcome to the *casa*. Now you have your own key," she said.

New Year's Eve arrived and left in virtual silence. Fireworks seemed inappropriate in the wake of the Waffle Barn. Roy and Ellie spent the evening sipping champagne after dinner and then waited for the Times Square ball to fall on television. They cheered and clinked glasses when the New York crowd shouted, "HAPPY NEW YEAR."

Roy and Ellie shared their own "happy new year's" and a deep kiss. Then she got on her knees before him. Ellie unbuckled his belt and unzipped his pants.

"Time for another lesson," she said.

---

The next morning, Roy was nudged from his sleep by birds joyfully welcoming a new dawn. He rolled onto his back, and Ellie almost instinctively nestled her head on his shoulder, her arm across his chest. He peered at the ceiling, imagining a mirror. His anger at his comrades for leaving him behind had dissipated. The despair and loneliness he initially felt and been replaced by something else … a feeling of home.

# CHAPTER 22

The new year was but a few days old when Anton returned to his fieldwork, checking off his self-made promise to visit Arkabutla Lake. The reservoir had been created in 1940 with the construction of the Arkabutla Dam on the Coldwater River. There were rivers on Xylodon, but not any that would rival the major waterways on Earth. Human-constructed dams were of high interest to Xylodonian scientists and those in the governing class.

Anton noticed some minnows playing in the shallows as he walked along the shoreline. He made a note to inquire as to whether aquatic life forms outside plants should be collected. He went a few steps further, then heard a whimpering sound. It may have been a cry for help or for mourning. He stopped and listened. Quiet. Anton started to proceed, but then heard the sound again. Then he heard the slightest rustling.

He walked over to some bushes and said, "Hello. Hello." The whimpering came again, but to his right. Anton looked behind a tree and spotted a grocery sack. The sound seemed to be coming from there. There was a slight movement as well.

Anton peered into the sack. The bottom was filled with dark-haired dog pups, none of them moving. Except one, barely visible

## CHAPTER 22

under the rest. This one was the source of that somber sound. Anton carefully lifted the pup out of the sack and placed it inside his jacket to warm up. "Easy now. You're safe," Anton told the shivering creature, eyes barely open.

He grabbed a hand spade from his kit and buried the pup's brothers and sisters. Six of them.

Anton tucked his jacket into his pants to keep the pup from falling out and dashed to his scooter. He knew of a veterinary clinic in Hernando and made for it as fast as his vehicle would allow.

The pup was greeted by the veterinary staff with ooh's and ahh's and was rushed into an examination room. Anton, now Roy, explained the circumstances behind the pup's discovery to the veterinarian.

"Sadly, I've seen it happen way too many times. People get a dog, don't get it spayed and then they can't feed the pups," said the doctor. "Sad. Sad. Sad. This fella is about six weeks old. Looks like a chiweenie. A Chihuahua-dachshund mix."

"Can you help this little guy?" Roy asked.

"I think I can. He's malnourished. Look how skinny he is. And he's suffering from exposure. I'm guessing whatever warmth he got from the other pups saved his life. And you, of course. Let's take a look at him in the back. You can wait here."

Roy passed the time learning about dog breeds from the charts on the wall. After about an hour, the veterinarian returned with the pup squirming in his hands. "I think he's gonna be OK. We've done all we can for him. Gave him some soft food to eat. Cleaned him up. There are no injuries. We can't keep him though. We're full up."

Roy took the pup and thanked the doctor, who gave him some instructions for further care. He bought a small carrier—one of the nurses gave him an old towel to line the bottom with—and paid the bill.

He rode over to Ellie's, who was still on holiday break. "I got you a late Christmas present," he said, opening the carrier. "Hope you like it."

"Omigosh, he's so tiny," she shrieked.

"Found him out in the woods. The vet says he's going to be OK."

"He was out in the woods?"

"Somebody left him in a sack with six other pups. They didn't make it."

Ellie looked at him. "Six?"

"Yeah, they …." Then Roy caught the connection she was making. "Yes, six."

Ellie cooed over the small furball. "Well, he's got a home now. What should we name him?"

They pondered for a moment before both pounced on the obvious answer. "Gator," they said.

## CHAPTER 23

Ellie's comparison of Gator's six siblings to the Waffle Barn percolated in Anton's mind for several days. The memories were like a butcher's shop slicer, trimming a bit of his soul with each revolution. He tried to replace the dark visions clouding his mind with happier thoughts. Ellie's smile. Baby Gator's frolicking. The trip to Memphis. The Marlo Thomas ad at the movie theater.

Memphis.

Suddenly, an idea came to him.

---

Ellie could not be involved in this. He fashioned an excuse about having some experiments to complete and reports to write. "Just for one night," he told her. She made a whimpering sound. Gator joined the sorrowful choir. "Lord, not the both of you."

Roy went back to the RV in Eudora and waited until well after midnight before hopping on his scooter and headed up I-55 toward Memphis. About halfway there he paused to review his preparations. He had entered some information into the GPS feature on his watch, which then directed him to his destination.

There it is, he said. Danny Thomas Boulevard. The area was generally familiar to him, but the dark complicated full recognition.

He didn't turn into the hospital campus, opting to park the scooter across the way near Winchester Park. He then began walking along a roadway called St. Jude's Place that took him into the heart of the facility. Signs led him to a series of sidewalks and eventually to one of the dorm-like buildings where child patients resided during their treatment.

Now here's the tricky part, he thought, staying in the shadows outside. He had done some computer research over the past few days on the current roster of St. Jude's physicians. *Ah. Here's a good one*, he told himself, tapping the photo of oncologist Miguel Rosario. Anton stored the image in the memory of his holo-biometrometer.

Now, outside this St. Jude's dorm, Anton called up Rosario's image and tapped his "watch." Instantly he took on the image of Dr. Rosario. He reached into a coat pocket and pulled out a stethoscope, which he draped around his neck. *Got to look the part*, he told himself. The doors swooshed open as he walked in.

A night nurse looked up from the admissions station. "Oh. Hello Dr. Rosario. A bit late for you, isn't it?" the nurse said.

He waved a hand. "Couldn't sleep. I got worried about a patient. Something I need to check on their chart."

"No problem. Good to see you." The engrossed nurse went back to her computer screen, and he went down the nearest hall.

Anton suspected there were cameras recording his movement, but he wasn't concerned if this guise held, and there was no reason it shouldn't. He paused outside a patient's room. "Krissy Middleton. Age eight. Dubuque, Iowa," he whispered to himself.

He entered Krissy's room, prepared with a cover story about performing routine checks if the child was awake or if parents were present. He was in luck; Krissy was sleeping soundly. A bandanna was around her head.

Anton used his holo-biometrometer to perform a scan on the

## CHAPTER 23

child and received a diagnosis within seconds. Acute Myeloid Leukemia. He turned a dial on his watch and allowed it to perform another scan that emitted a greenish light that eventually turned yellow, then blue, then stopped. He turned, cracked the door slightly to peek both ways, and left the room.

Anton/Rosario then slipped quietly into the room of Devontae Washington, age eleven, of Buffalo, New York. Thyroid cancer. Unlike Krissy, Devontae had not quite crossed over into sleep. His eyelids were partly open, and he mumbled something as Anton approached. "Rosario" explained that he was simply doing some tests with a new device. The tests did not require him to be awake, he told the boy, who drifted off. Anton repeated the scans he had performed in Krissy's room.

Now, it was Daniel Morales' turn to get a visit from the familiar stranger. Daniel was five and from Taos, New Mexico, and had Hodgkin's Lymphoma. He was wearing Garanimals pajamas and was tightly clutching a teddy bear. Daniel never moved as the strange lights enveloped him.

Next came Jessie Chambers, nine, from Slayton, Minnesota. She had liver cancer. Jessie apparently liked to draw and finger paint; there was evidence of her artwork all about the room. "Rosario" came to her bedside. *Let the light show begin*, he said to himself, pleased that there was no reaction from Jessie.

Anton left the room, but now approached a corner that led to a series of more patient rooms. He took a couple steps into the darkened corridor but halted when he saw a nurse and security guard at the far end of the hall. The pair were whispering animatedly to one another and hadn't seen him. He backed into the first hallway and set his "watch" to stealth mode. He was now virtually invisible.

Anton stood quietly, and the two chatty Cathys walked past. He waited until they were well clear, and he then advanced into the new hallway. He became Dr. Rosario once more.

He entered the room of Zoe Harris, age eight from Paducah, Texas. Her chart indicated she had multiple myeloma, caused when plasma cells become cancerous with bone or tissue. She was fighting three tumors. Zoe's room was adorned with paper hearts and balloons, almost enough to carry her bed away. "Rosario" approached the slumbering child, clad in Lily Pulitzer pajamas, and hit his watch. Scan. Treat. Review. Anton again exercised his "caution routine" before going to the next room.

Anton soft-stepped into the room of Vihaan Singh of Tarpon Springs, Florida. The seven-year-old was suffering from Retinoblastoma, a cancer that attacks the retina. His eyes were covered with a gauze bandage. Anton repeated the process with the holo-biometrometer, which took barely more than a minute to complete. He looked out, and the halls were clear.

He tried to stay in the shadows as much as possible as he approached the main reception area. Summoning his "tired and harried doctor" voice, he hurried past the admissions desk. "All good. G'night," he said, not turning to look at the nurse.

"G'night yourself, Dr. Rosario. Drive safe," she replied, only briefly looking up.

Outside the dorm, into the shadows he went once more, this time transitioning to his Roy appearance. The entire "mission" inside the facility had taken less than forty-five minutes. Roy felt jubilation on several levels, but it was also a moment of rationalization. He knew his actions could be considered interference and a serious regulatory violation by Xylodonian command. But he weighed that against the image of six humans slaughtered at Waffle Barn and against six lifeless pups trapped in a sack.

As Anton walked back to his scooter, he felt each of these emotions churning against one another. But as he got on his scooter, the positive prevailed. Suddenly, he felt lighter.

---

The next morning—with Roy still solidly asleep—Krissy Middleton awoke and looked about her room. It has become cliché to say one "bounds" out of bed—how does one bound out of a bed anyway? But today, Krissy felt bound for something somewhere. Still in her

## CHAPTER 23

pajamas, she scoot-scooted down the hall to the admissions desk. Still too small to be seen, she called out, "Hello! Anyone there?"

The nurse stood up and looked over the top of the desk. Her mouth fell agape.

Krissy stood looking up at her with big blue eyes, but that is not what stunned the nurse. All of Krissy's blonde curls had come back.

"I'm hungry," said Krissy. "Got pancakes?"

## CHAPTER 24

Over the next forty-eight hours or so, the headlines reverberated across Memphis and much of the nation. "MEMPHIS MIRACLE" read both CNN and the Memphis Commercial Appeal. "6 CANCER KIDS CURED OVERNIGHT," bellowed the New York Post. There were variations across all forms of news media. Social media hummed at high speed.

The cameras could not get enough of Krissy, DeVontae, Danny, Zoe, Vihaan, and Jessie after their cancers were found to have gone into complete remission. Their doctors were also stunned to find evidence that all the children's hair had started to grow back. When asked by reporters about the overnight development, the St. Jude doctors were at a loss to provide an explanation. Yes, they had high hopes for some of the new treatments and therapies—but nothing like this was expected.

Krissy was asked by a local TV reporter where she wanted to go eat after having hospital food for so long. "IHOP!" she yelled. Naturally, it became a meme.

No one was more shocked by the turn of events than Dr. Miguel Rosario, the real one. When he got out of his car in the St. Jude's parking lot he was greeted by a phalanx of cameras and micro-

## CHAPTER 24

phones. The flummoxed physician denied any involvement but could not offer any viable explanation for what had been captured on hospital cameras. His wife vouched that he was at home asleep at the time the miracle worker was making his rounds.

Rosario pointed to blow-ups of hospital security footage as support. "Look at the watch on this man's left wrist. I don't even wear a watch," he said at a news conference. None of the hospital officials could explain how "Dr. Rosario" was there one moment, but then gone with the nurse and security guard walked by. A glitch in the software was the best explanation they could come up with.

That did little to still the waters. Conspiracies clad in spiritual overtones of all shapes and sizes abounded. Some from the political extreme postulated that the event had been faked to distract from whatever was currently bedeviling the White House.

Meanwhile, the parents of still ailing children at St. Jude's wondered through their tears why their child wasn't chosen.

That, and other questions, could not be answered. At least, not at that time anyway.

## CHAPTER 25

The next Saturday was a lazy one. Roy looked in amusement as Gator pulled on the laces of his sneaker, making little growly noises. Ellie was entranced by the latest St. Jude's follow-up on her iPad.

"Can you believe this Memphis story? And we were just up there a few weeks ago. It says here the kids are already starting to go home. Finally, some good news for a change."

"Yeah," replied Roy. "And did you notice?"

"Notice what?"

"Your number six came up again. Six Waffle Barn victims. Six puppies. Six cured kids."

Ellie looked at him open-mouthed. "You're right." Then she emulated the music from "The Twilight Zone" theme. "Dee-doo, dee-doo, dee-doo, dee-doo."

Given that show's fetish for coincidence, it was the perfect theme tune for the moment, Roy thought. Besides, it sounded enchanting coming from Ellie.

Roy told Ellie that he had to run some errands that afternoon, plus he needed some fresh clothes if they were going out that night. "Fine. I've got some grading to do anyway. I'll be hungry

## CHAPTER 25

around six, so don't be late," she said, giving him a goodbye peck.

Roy, indeed, needed some clean attire, but he made a stop along the way at the Eudora cemetery. He parked his scooter and walked among the headstones. Sunlight fought its way through the tree limbs, creating a checkerboard mixture of light and shadow. This is what folks mean when they use the word "dappled," Roy thought. The watered grass was still dewy in the late morning, and all was quiet except for a gaggle of attendant birds.

After a short but reverent search, he came upon the headstone he was looking for:

*Ezra "Gator" Hopkins.*
*1926—2023.*
*Navy veteran. Builder. Teller of tales.*
*A finer friend you will never have.*

Ezra's tombstone was coupled with one for his wife, Lillian. A rose was engraved into her headstone.

"Lillian. I'm so sorry, Ezra. I never thought to ask for your wife's name. I was too enthralled with your stories to delve into the real you. There was so much I could have asked, should have asked," Roy said to his friend. "There was so much I could have learned from you. There was much that this *girgach* nation could have learned from you. You were a witness to history. You were not afraid to stand against great evil. With your hands you built homes, you built a life. I miss your laugh, your old shirts and your wit, with its equal opportunity belligerence. No one was spared. Most of all, I miss my friend. You had a full life, but you were taken too soon.

"Oh, what does *girgach* mean? I never got a chance to tell you. I'm not really from around these parts. I'm from someplace far, far away. That's a bit of a hint, by the way. Well, *girgach* is a term you like used quite a bit in the Navy. Let's leave it at that.

"I owe you a big thank you, my friend. Thanks for introducing me to Ellie. There was an emptiness in my life I hadn't noticed until she came around. She's helped with the new emptiness that arrived when you left. She means a great deal to me. We got a puppy not long after the Waffle Barn happened. We named him after you.

Gator, not Ezra. I don't know of any dogs that would come running to Ezra.

"OK, I will come clean and just tell you. I am not from your world—literally and figuratively—but I have tried to see it through your eyes. You were a believer in justice, and you would have wanted something positive to come from your death. That's what I tried to do. I gave back life to six children suffering from dreadful diseases. One life restored for each one taken that terrible day at Waffle Barn. That's my epitaph to you, Ezra.

"Now, I know what you are going to say, you cantankerous old cuss. 'Why didn't you do more? Why stop at six?' I had my reasons, time being chief among them. But there's more I might do; more I hope to do.

"Speaking of that, what are your thoughts on this, old friend?" asked Roy, taking a wrinkled bit of newspaper out of a pocket. "Just listen. A California man was arrested recently with nearly 250 guns in his home. He had more than a million rounds of ammunition. A million rounds. Among the weapons were eleven machine guns and sixty assault rifles. He also had some grenades.

"I've read this over and over. I can't wrap my head around it. This man had enough weapons to arm two companies of soldiers. How does that happen? Why does someone need 250 guns? How can one person buy 250 guns and someone in authority not notice? Don't they care? I can just imagine what you'd say, old friend. 'It's to make up for his tiny pecker.' Yes, that would be something you'd say. And you'd probably be right. But I bet you would also say it had something to do with fear. In your words, 'great big buckets' of fear.

"So, about that fear. I'm asking your permission to try something. If it works, perhaps there will no longer be a reason to fear. If it doesn't, well, no harm will be done.

"I hope you are watching down on me, old friend. I wish for you calm seas wherever you are sailing now. I miss our chats. I will be back soon."

Roy then walked away. You couldn't see it, but something heavy lay on his shoulders.

## CHAPTER 26

Ellen Atkinson may have thought the "Memphis Miracle" was wonderful news, but it was just the sort of thing that made Sub-Protector Korphan curious. And nervous. And furious. All at the same time.

Several of the other Xylodonian surveillance teams had passed the information along to their contacts in space, more as an unusual informational bauble than a cause for concern. Another reason the Memphis incident raised eyebrows was speculation in some circles that humans might have made technological advances in health care. An improvement of this degree was deemed unlikely but worth noting and monitoring.

But Korphan was skeptical that this "miracle" was human made. He checked his maps and saw that Eudora, Mississippi, was in close proximity to the hospital where the extraordinary event had occurred. He placed a call to Termas.

"Hello, Termas. How is Zephyra doing?" he began.

"As well as can be expected, sir. She's due any day now," Termas replied.

"That's excellent news. I hope things go well. Do you know the gender of the child?"

"It will be a male, sir."

"Excellent, excellent. You and Zephyra must be very proud," said Korphan. "Listen. The reason I am calling is, one, I wanted to check up on you and Zephyra, but secondly, I also need some information. About Anton-7."

"Anton, sir? Has he returned?"

"No … not yet. I have an incident report I am looking into about something that occurred near your last Earth base of operations. In a place called Memphis."

"What sort of incident, sir?"

"Six Earth children were suddenly cured of terminal diseases. All in one night. It's not the sort of thing Earth technology is ready to accommodate, am I correct?"

"Yes, sir. That would be the case as far as I know."

"What does Anton know about this place called Memphis? Did any of your team go there? It's not far from where you were based."

"No, sir, we never went there. At least Zephyra and I never did. Anton would go out into the countryside to collect plants for our cover story, but he never went as far as Memphis that I know of."

"Now, be frank with me. Do you think Anton would have had something to do with this? He knows that such interference is forbidden under Xylodonian regulations, correct?"

"Yes, sir. I mean, no sir," stammered Termas. "What I mean is, he knows the regulations manual backward and forward. He rarely interacted with humans during our tour. So, I don't think this would be any of his doing."

"Since you and I are in agreement that this incident appears to be beyond human technology, do you have any other explanation as to why six dying children are suddenly back playing ball with their friends?"

There was a long pause. Termas started to delve into the supposed powers of Earth deities but decided against it. "No, sir, I do not."

"And while we're speaking, how are you progressing on those pregnancy guidelines for the training manual I asked you to create?"

## CHAPTER 26

"Coming along, sir. I'm almost ready to submit them to you."

"Fine, fine. Well then, please let me know when the infant arrives. Good luck to you and Zephyra."

He hung up. Korphan placed another call. "Give me the head of Guardian training, please."

## CHAPTER 27

By the middle of January, Ellie had returned to her classroom. Roy spent more of his days at the RV, but he would drop by her house to give snacks to Gator and take him out to do his business. During one of his visits, while Gator was sniffing for the proper location in the backyard, Roy picked up Ellie's iPad. Emulating Ellie's fingerprint to unlock the device was no challenge.

He was intrigued by the icon for an application called Associated Press. Most of his Earth news came from the television, not from the print or digital formats. But he was curious; might as well get some intel while I'm here, he thought.

He thumbed through the stories of carnage from across the nation. Weekend shootings in Chicago set a record. An eighty-four-year-old white man shoots a Black kid who knocked on his door. A Minneapolis police officer shoots a motorist reaching for his phone. Two teen-agers killed in Los Angeles gang violence. The common denominator in these disparate cases was easy to distill—guns, guns, guns. Guns, swirling in a cauldron of hate and fear.

Xylodon had advanced past such mindless violence centuries ago. Only the Guardians, under the meticulous supervision of the

# CHAPTER 27

Protectorate, were allowed lethal armaments and those were kept secure until deemed needed. Xylodonian temperament and tradition played key roles—angry outbursts or divisive speech, common occurrences on Earth, would lead to social disdain and a figurative banishment on Anton's planet. Yes, there were "states" of a kind, but they existed primarily because of geographic necessity. The central government oversaw a harmonious distribution of resources that kept disputes at a minimum.

Those on Anton's world were guided by the logic and the notion that cooperation was the preferred path to achievement. That was not to say that on occasion there were those who violated societal rules. The consequences were severe—banishment to Xylodon's third moon, where the banished were left to their own devices to survive. Rehabilitation, as determined by the judiciary of the Confluence Council, could lead to a return to Xylodon. Generally, these rare crimes involved putting self before fellow members of Xylodon society. Theft. Fraud. Financial conspiracy. Terms like massacre, serial killer, and mass murder did not exist.

Roy closed his eyes and imagined Ezra on the cold Waffle Barn floor, his body still amid the blood and shattered glass. He had left the scene without seeing the bodies, but he read later about the terrible capabilities of an AR-15. It was not the peaceful ending Ezra deserved. There should be no more Waffle Barns, he told himself.

He returned to the RV, wallowing in his thoughts. What he couldn't grasp was that one of America's most revered laws had opened the door to wanton bloodshed for decades upon decades. The Second Amendment seemed simple enough, after all it was only twenty-seven words. The amendment was ratified after America's revolt against Britain. The new nation stood upon shaky legs; the need for militias to supplement the military was understandable. But interpretations of the amendment evolved. Over the years it was determined that any single person could be a "militia." The term "well-regulated" became anathema in some political circles. With "regulation" lost amid a never-ending debate—with the legal battalions of James Madison continually losing ground to those of George Mason—any type of weapon could now find its way to a store shelf.

The Second Amendment had become like the snake swallowing its own tail.

Instead of preserving peace, the cancerous laws that had sprung from interpretations of the Second Amendment had become roadblocks to that peace, Anton concluded. A tug-of-war raged within his convictions. Duty vs. right.

He smiled. If one person could be a militia, then one person could be a "Supreme Court." Some kind of demonstration seemed to be necessary. One with enough shock value to recalibrate a planet. One that might make Ezra evoke his barrel laugh.

The seed of an idea took root.

## CHAPTER 28

Anton outlined his plan on a legal pad, which he stored in a safe within the RV. He created a checklist, marking off the items after completion.

His first task was making alterations and improvements to the antenna array atop the vehicle. He was fortunate—most of what he couldn't find in the RV's storage he was able to procure from area electronics and hardware stores. He had to go to Jackson to buy a pair of cellphone signal-booster, much pricier than an FM radio booster, but much more powerful. The cellphone boosters were illegal in some places, but they would be well disguised by the time Anton was done with them. He was able to easily adapt them to meet his needs. *Good thing I wasn't always a botanist*, Anton thought.

In theory, the improvisations would extend the array's reach many times more than at present. It would require some testing to determine just how powerful it had become. Operation of the array would usually have to be done manually, but his Xylodonian computer system could arrange for a signal emission that would remain constant as long as the energy supply held. He would have to hope that any outages would be short-lived. What Anton needed now was a "Wifi booster" of sorts, something that could travel with him but maintain contact with the array. He fashioned a "booster" that fit in the crown of a ring, but his testing revealed shortcomings in power. A second ring proved a satisfactory bridge.

He put on the two rings, which provoked memories of an Earth author named Tolkien. "One ring to rule them all ... but a second ring to bind them." But I don't recall Tolkien ever writing about a watch, Anton mused. That's the key to this mission to Mordor.

Anton felt ready. He asked Jonnie Barnes to keep an eye on the RV and his scooter. He then arranged a flight from Memphis to Washington's Ronald Reagan National Airport for two days from now, and he booked a room in a moderately priced hotel in the D.C. suburbs.

Then there was Ellie to deal with.

Later that day, Roy greeted her with a hearty hug and spun her around. Then he cuddled Gator in his arms.

"I have some bad news, so let me get it out of the way before we have dinner," he said.

"Oh, no. What's up?"

"I have been called to D.C. to give a presentation on the aquatic plants I have been studying and the effects of climate change."

"Oh, that's not so bad. I'm surprised you haven't had to go to Washington before now."

"Yeah, me too. But so far, they have been happy with the PDF reports I've been sending them," he said, figuratively crossing his fingers behind his back. "Now I have to give a PowerPoint to some international muckity-mucks who are visiting."

"Wow, look at you. How long will you be gone?"

"About three days."

Ellie stuck out her bottom lip and mimicked a Gator whimper. Roy laughed and kissed her nose.

"Are you flying out of Memphis?" she asked, and he nodded. "Need a ride?"

"Would love one, otherwise I'll have to Uber" Roy said. No way I'm taking the scooter again, he thought. "But don't you have to teach that day?"

"I feel a sick day coming on," she said. "Cough, cough."

## CHAPTER 28

*Flight day. January 23*

Roy scootered over to Ellie's house using tiedowns to hold his overnight bag and briefcase. After tending to Gator's needs, they got into the Tesla and were soon Memphis-bound.

Ellie noticed Roy was not as chatty as usual and called him out. "Why so quiet, Plant Boy?"

"I'm just going over my presentation in my head. I don't want to embarrass myself," he said. It was only a partial fib. Details kept circulating, but they had nothing to do with aquatic plants. He reached for her right hand and gripped it. That seemed to appease her.

She dropped him off at the American Airlines entrance, and he collected his bag and briefcase. She had never seen him with a briefcase before.

"My, don't you look all professional and such," she cooed. "All you need is a hat, and you could be on 'Mad Men'."

Whatever that was, Roy wondered. "My return flight's still up in the air, so don't worry about picking me up. I can Uber."

"If I'm free, I'd be glad to do it."

"I'm not too keen on you driving alone at night," Roy countered sincerely.

"OK. Well, give us a kiss, and I'll see you when I see you."

Roy's long embrace and provocative kiss had her swooning.

"You sure you have to go? Something seems to be rising, and I don't mean grandma's biscuits."

"You're so bad. I will call or text you when I get settled."

Roy waved as she drove off then entered the facility. He had never flown on an Earth aircraft before, but thus he began the airline passenger's painful gantlet. Ticket desk, ID. Boarding pass. Checking luggage? No. Security line. Boarding pass. Shoe removal. Bag bins (Roy included his watch just in case). X-ray scan. Hands above your head. Battle competing bins to retrieve your valuables. Get shoes back on before being run over.

Having survived the TSA's hurdles and challenges, he rewarded himself with a coffee and a cinnamon roll. Afterward, he settled into the gate area to await his flight. Roy flipped through his cellphone notifications to pass the time. He stopped scrolling. "Ex-Worker Kills 5 At Indiana Auto Plant" headlined a news alert that was thirty minutes old.

His focus returned to his mission.

## CHAPTER 29

Anton had selected a Hilton Garden Inn conveniently located within walking distance of a Metrorail station for his stay in the D.C. area. The flight from Memphis had been uneventful, save for the infant placed a seat ahead of him who fouled his diaper just before landing. Because the seat belt light was on, the child's parent had to wait to change him. Anton recoiled at the smell, which pervaded much of the coach section, and mentally crossed off having children in the future.

Even in January, Reagan Airport seemed busy. There were unexpected waits to secure an Uber to take him to suburban Maryland. He had an additional wait at the hotel check-in—an underdressed couple from Florida picked that moment to search their luggage for their coats. Once the typical hotel desk bureaucracy was out of the way, he grabbed a water bottle and some tourist maps before heading to his room. A king-size bed never looked so inviting, he told himself.

After reaching his comfort zone, he ordered room service and called Ellie to fill her in on the day's events. She chortled over the poopy baby story. A knock at his door ended their call. His steak was a skosh on the tough side and his baked potato was barely warm, but the meal satisfied his nutrient needs. He spread out the tourist maps on the bed and looked over his notes. Tomorrow was to be used as a scouting day. Thursday was the main event. After a shower and a little television, he turned off the light and closed his eyes.

---

*Wednesday, January 24*

Anton arose early and went to the Metrorail station. Once aboard, he sat by himself, alone in his thoughts as American suburbia whizzed by outside the train window. A few small, lingering doubts about his mission tried to be heard above the train's rumble-rumble, much like Ellie's students raising their hands in class. But Anton found himself caught within a fervent momentum, one that was necessary and wouldn't be denied. Would he be forgiven? Would it even matter?

He continued to use his Roy appearance as he traveled into the American capital. He had selected the Foggy Bottom-GWU station as his stopping point; it was the nearest to the Lincoln Memorial and other tourist sites he had found among the hotel maps.

His cellphone buzzed. It was a text from Ellie. *Good luck with your presentation today!* (kiss emoji)

*Good morning! Thanks! I will need it. Talk soon* (heart emoji), he tapped back.

He climbed the Lincoln Memorial steps and started intently at the great man. Lincoln's bony knees jutted from his seat. Anton/Roy searched Lincoln's face, particularly the eyes, to see if there was evidence of what he might be thinking about modern America. No answer came.

Washington was considered a Southern city, but there was a biting chill that Anton found a bit comforting. It also kept the crowds down. He walked over to the Korean War Memorial, with its nineteen stoic figures patrolling ... what? What was before them? Anton wondered. What came after? He looked in their eyes as well. Cold. Frozen with images of things young men should never see.

He had a similar feeling when he ventured over to the Vietnam

## CHAPTER 29

War Memorial, a journey in and of itself. One begins on higher ground, with but a relatively small number of names engraved on the black wall. As one travels downward, the sections of the wall grow as does the names of the fallen. Eventually one is swallowed by the immenseness of the butcher's bill of this war. Along the way, he saw the flowers and notes crammed into the memorial's crevices. Other mementos were placed at various spots along its base. The memorial bore the names of more than 58,000 killed during America's involvement over fourteen years, give or take. There were no words given there for any single name, but each told a story.

As he moved along, he saw the Jefferson Memorial in the distance through the bare branches of the cherry trees. Another great man who envisioned greater. He paused to visit the Martin Luther King Jr. Memorial, dedicated to the man whose bloodstains he had seen in Memphis. King had stirred thousands, perhaps millions, with a speech given near this very spot. Arms crossed. What was in his eyes? Was it defiance? Or was it hope? Anton was uncertain.

Lincoln. Jefferson. King. What was learned from their lessons?

Near this site, a much lesser man gave a self-serving speech that was antithetical to the words of the great men standing here. Rightfully, there were no monuments to him. What was that lesson?

Anton walked past yet another monument to yet another great man—the Washington Monument. Its construction—interrupted by America's Civil War—was perhaps an unintended symbol of that conflict. Because different quarries were used, the lower part of the statue was built with slightly darker stones, the top sections feature lighter stones. The light overcoming the bitter dark. Anton wondered if the top of the obelisk should be dark once more.

His quick lunch was a hot dog and lemonade from a food vendor. He moved along with an unanswered curiosity as he entered a granite valley of the nation's great museums and galleries. Another time, perhaps, Anton thought. My destination is in view.

*Wednesday afternoon*

Anton crossed Second Street and gave a mental salute to the famed general, Ulysses S. Grant, taking note of a row of portable restrooms servicing tourists and nearby construction workers. He approached the U.S. Capitol Plaza and Visitor Entrance, pausing to take in the Capitol Dome and the Statue of Freedom atop it. He joined a tour group and was led inside; there were no longer metal detectors placed to slow their entry. The ruling House party had seen to that.

The group marched upon Emancipation Hall, half absorbing the tour guide's tired retelling of history. Eventually, they were taken to the spectacular Rotunda with its artwork and Crypt and its entrancing view of the dome's interior. The tour ended, at least for Anton, in the muted sunlight within Statuary Hall.

Anton went into a restroom and let his watch work its magic. Now invisible, he then entered the House side of the Capitol, intent on familiarizing himself with the location of a certain hearing room. The exterior of the Capitol, with its well-ordered structure, belies a maddening maze of official warrens and dens within. Anton spent almost forty-five minutes on scouting mission, remarkably able to avoid humans in the busy building. Once satisfied, he found another restroom and returned to Roy mode.

After leaving the Capitol, he stopped at a Mall souvenir stand and bought a few items that might be useful tomorrow. He found something for Ellie as well.

He trudged back to Foggy Bottom station under graying skies. Within an hour, he was back in his hotel room and sitting at the desk to make notes and create his own map.

Then it was time to check in with Ellie.

---

Meanwhile, Jonnie Barnes was doing some checking of his own. Earlier that day, he had seen a UPS truck make a delivery to Roy's RV, leaving three packages on the steps.

After dark, he drove over to the odd-looking RV and quickly put the packages in the back of his truck. He drove to a nearby dirt road and got out a flashlight.

Jonnie tore open the packages and looked in. It was nothing but

## CHAPTER 29

office supplies and some glass containers, the kind commonly found in a lab.

*Hell. Not much here. Maybe I could make a beer mug out of this,* he told himself, lofting a beaker. As he perused over the objects, his thumb and forefinger ensnared an angry pimple on his jawline. He squeezed and then wiped the eruption on his jeans. Seeing the blood on his finger gave him a thought.

*I wonder what little Betsy will be wearing tonight?*

## CHAPTER 30

*Thursday, January 25*

The city was abuzz that morning. The day of the big showdown on Capitol Hill had arrived. Confrontation is a potent political tool, especially when you can use your cherry-picked media to spin the outcome any way you want.

Heather Brisbane, the ne'er-do-well daughter of Jackson Brisbane, the U.S. ambassador to Britain, would be answering a subpoena to appear before the House Committee on Oversight and Accountability. Heather Brisbane, who had long ago decided to favor party over just about everything else, had been surviving on her surname in the decade after somehow graduating from college.

Those among the majority-party members of the committee had questions about loans between father and his scandal-plagued daughter that might have involved overseas funding or might indicate favoritism by a lending institution. There was no real evidence of wrongdoing but such things matter little in a kangaroo court when the cameras are rolling. One of the primary witnesses against her was found to be an agent of a foreign government and had fled the U.S., nowhere to be found. Another witness had been indicted on charges of lying to the FBI. Still, the show must go on.

# CHAPTER 30

Sleep had been fleeting for Anton. He awoke early, put on his suit and overcoat, grabbed his briefcase, and took the train into the city. This time, still in the guise of Roy, he disembarked at the Capitol South station, about a ten-minute walk from the Capitol. He found a change machine within the station and slid in a couple of bills.

He found an empty portable potty, secured the door and set down his briefcase. It smelled awful. *Offal,* chuckled Anton. *I will have to use that one on Ellie.* He set his watch to personal stealth mode and tapped. Now invisible to humans, he had only to wait until the proper moment to open the door without attracting much notice. Peering through the door slats, he was able to leave the container just before the odor choked him.

The immediate challenge would be to avoid physical contact with humans to, first, enter the Capitol and then find and use the route he had scouted the day before. This is where the coins came in. To get past the security area, or to avoid contact, Anton carefully tossed a few coins on the floor. It was an unmistakable sound that humans, especially Americans, reacted to quickly. Even Capitol Police officers couldn't hold back from joining these providential coin hunts. It was particularly helpful for Anton when squealing children jousted with one another on the floor over nickels and dimes.

Avoiding mishap, Anton was able to find the same House-side restroom he had used the day before. He entered an empty stall and disengaged from stealth mode. He then found a more suitable appearance, one that he had selected the night before, and put it into play. His hair became thinner and whiter, and he had a matching mustache and goatee. Age spots dotted his face and hands. Anton opened his briefcase and took out some accoutrements—silk handkerchief, coat pin, tie tack—to give his suit a more expensive sheen. He also took out his two rings, placing one on each ring finger.

Anton walked out and approached the hearing room doors, recalling an Earth biblical tale. *As the prophet Daniel would say, it's now or never.*

# CHAPTER 31

"All righty, let's have quiet in the chamber," bellowed "Big Jim" Cowley, banging a gavel loudly to herd reporters, photographers and visitors into their places.

Cowley, of Kentucky, was chairman of the powerful House Oversight Committee. The panel—which has the power to investigate, well, almost anything it considers to be under its jurisdiction—has forty-seven members. In addition to the chairman, there is a ranking member who chieftains the minority party members. The committee includef twenty-five members from the majority party and twenty from the minority party, the latter often entering the fray with one arm tied behind its back. For example, the minority members could not exercise subpoena power unless granted by the majority.

The majority members, after weeks of legal brawling, had finally drawn Heather Brisbane into their spider's web. This hearing, they hoped, would be the casus belli, the beginning of a political domino theory that would sully her father, and by extension, the occupant of the White House. Heather, attorney at her side and looking like a small girl in her pale-yellow dress and pearls, was chum on the water.

Cowley then laid out the ground rules for the hearing. Each

## CHAPTER 31

member would have five minutes to ask questions, and the witness would have a like amount of time to answer. Members could "donate" their time to fellow members to complete a line of inquiry if desired. Photographers were told when they could perform their duties, and visitors were admonished to observe decorum.

"I will give an opening statement, which will be followed by one by the ranking member and then the witness will be allowed to give her opening statement," Cowley said. "I will then begin recognizing members for their questions."

The combatants then went into their respective corners.

Cowley began to bray about materials turned over to the committee by whistleblowers and suspicions created by a few dozen emails between one of Heather's business associates and her father. "For too long, there has been a shadow over her business activities. The American people are right to be concerned that the thousands of dollars that exchanged hands in foreign deals and mysterious bank loans are nothing more than blatant influence-peddling," he said. "Where is the transparency? We have a right to know. The American people have a right to know. Now, some have criticized this committee for not presenting sufficient evidence. Well, where there's smoke there's fire, and we are gonna get to the bottom of this raging inferno."

After Cowley concluded his statement, the ranking member, who had recently overcome a serious illness, pulled his microphone closer. "To quote the Bard: Oh, the slings and arrows of outrageous fortune. Yes, Ms. Brisbane has made money in business. Yes, some of that money came from overseas. How is that a crime? Is that not the American way? Again, we must point out that there is no evidence of wrongdoing here. The business associate in question was formerly a financial adviser to the ambassador. He helped prepare the ambassador's tax returns. Would they not exchange emails? Or is emailing now a crime?" he asked.

He continued, "I have three other points to make before I relinquish my time. One, Ms. Brisbane holds no elected or appointed office. She is allowed to make a profit. However, the former president's son-in-law, who was a White House adviser at the time, received billions from Saudi Arabia. Yet, no questions are asked by the majority. Two, several of these so-called whistleblowers have disappeared. One has reportedly fled the country. Three, Mr. Chairman, you gave your brother a loan that was substantially larger than the loan Ambassador Brisbane gave his daughter. Family loans are now a crime? Are we writing new law here?"

Cowley harumphed. "Let me remind the ranking member that this hearing is not about me, and whether or not our witnesses are physically present in this jurisdiction is immaterial. We have their testimony. It's all recorded."

It should have been Heather Brisbane's turn to speak, but the two politicians continued to spar. Amid the verbal fracas, Anton walked inro the chamber and approached the witness desk. He leaned over and told her attorney that a messenger bearing key documents was in the hallway. The excited lawyer moved quickly outside. Once the doors had shut, Anton sat in the empty chair. He opened the briefcase and took out a sheath of papers. He then gave each of his rings, one on each hand, a slight twist.

Heather Brisbane appeared startled and angled away. "Don't worry, Ms. Brisbane," Anton said. "I'm not here to harm you. I'm here to help."

Cowley finally gaveled in Heather to speak, knowing the traps he had set for this political Joan de Arc. But it was not her voice that was heard.

"Mr. Chairman, I will be speaking for Ms. Brisbane today," Anton said.

"This is most unusual. Please identify yourself, sir."

"My name is Radley Duvall. Some folks call me Boo."

"And what is your relationship with the witness?" Cowley asked.

"None, sir." The room began to murmur.

"None? Then why are you here? How did you get in here?"

Heather grabbed her microphone and belted out, "Mr. Chairman, I have never seen this man before in my life."

Anton calmed Heather with a hand on her shoulder. He took back the microphone.

## CHAPTER 31

"What is this? Some kind of ploy by the opposition?" Cowley shouted. "Officers, seize that man."

Four Capitol Police officers dashed toward the witness table, one reaching for some handcuffs. Radley pursed his lips and made a slight turn on his holo-biometrometer. The officers jolted to a halt.

In fact, everyone in the room was frozen in place. Except for Radley Duvall.

## CHAPTER 32

Between the score of lawmakers, dozens of scandal-weary journalists, and scores of rubber-necking visitors, there were perhaps three hundred people in the hearing chamber. They could speak, but they could not move. They were not in pain; they just could not control their limbs.

With his audience now captive, Radley became ringmaster.

"While there are many corners of this great land eagerly champing at the bit to see Ms. Brisbane reduced to tears, I am going to have to disappoint them," Radley said. "We have a much more important issue to talk about today."

Cowley snarled, struggling to move. Only the muscles above the shoulders would comply. "And just what do you think that is?"

"Guns," said Radley.

"GUNS?" shouted "Little Jim" Terkoff, the Ohio representative who was Cowley's primary confidante and whose surname was often accidentally mispronounced by his numerous critics. "What about guns? We don't have any authority over guns."

"Why, Representative Terkoff, this is the Oversight Committee, is it not? Aren't you supposed to oversee things? I know you folks have been busy naming post offices, but I would think you could

## CHAPTER 32

squeeze in a little oversight on something that's killing your children."

"Well, guns ain't one of them. That's covered by the Second Amendment," Terkoff said.

"How nice of you to bring up the Constitution," Radley said. "Aren't you one of the fellows who helped plot an insurrection? It's funny how you and your colleagues only seem to pay attention to the parts of that revered document that you agree with and discount the parts that counter your narrative. Like peaceful transfer of power and the Fourteenth Amendment."

As best they could, the minority members of the committee smirked and chuckled. Then a new voice took over. "Now, you listen here," said a scowling Margie Joye Blue of Georgia. "Who do you think you are? How dare you interrupt this hearing."

"How dare I, madam?" countered Radley, who began with a small lie. "As I came to the Capitol today, I passed a monument that bears the names of 58,000 young men and women who died at the behest of this nation's wishes. Those 58,000 deaths were recorded over a decade and a half. But just last year, 48,000 Americans died at the behest of guns. About half were suicides. It seems America is content to repeat a version of Vietnam year after year.

Radley stayed with the numbers. "If you do the math on that 48,000, that's a bit over 131 people killed each day by guns in the Land of Free and the Home of Brave. In the United Kingdom, they have 162 gun deaths per year. Per *year*. In Australia, it's 241 gun deaths per year. In Japan, it's 101. In New Zealand, it's forty-one per year. That's how dare I."

"The courts have ruled that people have the right to carry arms and not even conceal them," said another lawmaker, Rep. Lulu Babaloux of Colorado.

"That they have, madam. But these courts only follow the laws that Congress and legislatures enact," Radley said. "Look inside yourselves for a moment. Do you really think the nation's Founding Fathers had in mind a free rein on bump stocks, tactical vests, extended magazines, and dum-dum bullets when they wrote the Second Amendment? Did they really intend for teachers to be turned into security guards? Did they intend for abusive husbands to have access to guns? Did they intend for concealed and unconcealed weapons to be carried into schools, stores, and movie theaters? Do you think they intended to put vending machines for ammunition inside of stores? Including a hardware store in Texas right next to a middle school?"

"If someone had had a gun, they might have saved lives at that Aurora theater or that Littleton high school," Rep. Babaloux interjected.

"Or they might have killed bystanders in a darkened theater. Or they might have been mistaken by the police as being the perpetrator. Or, like the police, they may have found themselves outgunned by the killer."

Rep. Blue tendered an overused, stale-beer analysis. "We all know these shootings are nearly always a mental health issue. It's not a gun issue."

"Mental health is certainly something you know a little bit about, isn't it Rep. Blue?" Radley said. "Aren't you the one who suggested forest fires were caused by laser beams sent from space that are controlled by Jews? Aren't you the one who suggested the Capitol was patrolled by 'gazpacho' police? Lady, you put the 'pulse' in 'repulsive.'"

Blue's eyes shot daggers at the man giving witness.

Radley prodded further. "And, generally speaking, doesn't good mental health go hand in hand with being able to express empathy? Just recently, the supposed leader of your political party said that parents of slain children should 'get over it and move forward.' Where does that rank on your mental health scale?"

More eye daggers, but Radley easily evaded them.

"But, OK, let's explore the mental health issue for a moment if that's what you want. Who is checking on the mental health of a gun purchaser before the purchase? Adam Lanza killed twenty-six children and teachers at Sandy Hook in 2014. Salvador Ramos killed twenty-one at an elementary school in Uvalde, Texas, in 2022. Devin Kelley killed twenty-six people at a Texas church in 2017. That same year, Stephen Paddock murdered sixty people in Las Vegas. Robert

## CHAPTER 32

Card gunned down eighteen people in Maine just last fall. What did they all have in common? They all displayed mental health issues and other problems before each of these massacres.

"And they all were able to get a gun. And not just any gun. A weapon of war. And hundreds of rounds of ammunition without drawing any suspicion," Radley said to a suddenly hushed room. "Point. Click. Purchase. Boom … gun arrives a few days later. What checks were in place to stop these mentally diseased individuals? Whose responsibility is it to ensure those checks are effective? Apparently, it's not yours. You have forsaken the responsibility despite the desperate cries for help from those you took a vow to serve.

"OK then, let's play this out. Let's just look at the Uvalde slaughter, shall we? There were what, nearly four hundred police officers of different types outside the school against a lone gunman? Yet, they did nothing for seventy-seven minutes. The gunman was in a classroom with wounded children for seventy-seven minutes. Why? It wasn't a five-foot-eight kid the police were scared of; it was an AR-15. So much for 'the only way to stop a bad guy with a gun is by a good guy with a gun.' It appears what was needed was a good guy with some balls. Or a brain. Or both. Mental instability and AR-15s … my God, now there's a recipe for disaster."

"It's not the fault of the gun. It's the gun user. Besides, most people don't even know what the AR in AR-15 stands for. It's not 'assault rifle'," said Rep. Babaloux, in a proud-of-herself voice.

"Yes, it stands for Armalite. But that's hardly the point. Didn't you recently become a grandmother?" Radley asked. "What if your grandson had been at Columbine, or Sandy Hook, or Parkland, or Uvalde? Have you ever seen what an AR-15 round does to a child?"

Cowley, angry that he had not only lost control of the hearing but the day's message along with it, snapped, "This is not an issue that we can solve here today."

"No?" said Radley, eyebrows arched. "Well, if you don't have the resolve or moral courage to do something about it, perhaps I can."

"What do you mean?" said Cowley.

Radley adjusted each ring and then touched his "watch." It

hummed and a bluish glow enveloped the chamber. Radley counted the seconds; after a half-minute he tapped his watch.

"What just happened?" Cowley demanded.

"All of the guns in America are now gone," Radley said, smiling. "Well, not quite all of them. The military still has its weapons. But no civilian, not even the police, have guns now. Poof. Gone-ski. That includes that .32 revolver you had in your purse, Ms. Babaloux." She literally hissed.

Cowley looked at the four Capitol officers in the room. Their holsters were empty.

"What did you do? Where are their guns?" Cowley demanded.

"As I said. Gone. Now America will have a chance to be like Australia, New Zealand, Canada, and Norway after those countries confiscated guns or efficaciously banned weapons of war," Radley replied. "Think of it as being not so much 'The Day The Earth Stood Still,' but more like 'The Day That America Grew Up'."

A red-faced Margie Blue screamed at Radley, "Who do you think you are?"

"Who am I? Well, this may be difficult for you, but just think about it. How many people do you know can make other people freeze in place and make guns just disappear?"

The question seemed to be caught in a spin-cycle within the congresswoman's brain. After a few moments, her eyes widened, and her right hand was allowed to smack her forehead. "Oh, my God. You're JAY-ZUS! JAY-ZUS HAS COME BACK TO US! OH, MY LORD. OH, MY LORD. THIS MUST BE THE RAPTURE!!"

"Not quite. More like the Capture," said Radley, who suddenly stood, put his papers back into his briefcase and snapped it shut. "Have a good day, everyone."

Then he turned and walked right out the door.

## CHAPTER 33

A few seconds later, everyone in the room—and a few in the hallway—regained use of their limbs. Some tested their ability to move; Babaloux scoured her purse. No gun.

"Don't just stand there. Somebody go grab that man," shouted Cowley. The four officers present spoke urgently into their walkie-talkies, then they did as the chairman commanded.

Capitol Police and congressional aides soon flooded the House side of the Capitol. A few of those "frozen" outside the hearing chamber told officers that they saw a well-dressed gentleman turn down a nearby hallway. The officers went door to door, asking office occupants if they had a silver-haired, goateed man. None had.

At last, they came to the restrooms. A female officer opened the door to the women's restroom and looked inside. She squatted to view under the stalls. She looked at her comrades and shook her head.

Three of the male officers drew out their batons and burst into the men's room.

A small Black boy shouted in surprise. "Damn, ya'll. What ya'll want? I din't do nothin'." The boy was wearing a Washington

Commanders T-shirt and a Washington Nationals cap. He looked to be about ten or eleven years old.

As his colleagues searched the stalls, one of the officers asked the boy, "Son, did you see an older man in a suit come in here?"

"Nah, sir. I just did my business and was washin' my hands. Ain't seen nobody but ya'll."

"You sure, son?"

"Yassir. Just me in here with the roaches. Hey, is there a reward?"

The officer shook his head. "C'mon, guys. Must be another hallway."

The boy returned to washing his hands. He waited a few minutes, then left.

No one appeared to notice that the boy was standing next to a briefcase.

# CHAPTER 34

What happens when a nation that has an estimated four hundred million guns—more than one for each citizen—suddenly is thrown cold turkey off its lethal addiction?

Sheer, unadulterated, primal panic.

*Derek Bankston of Waterloo, Iowa, was one of thousands of gun store owners who saw their entire inventory just disappear. Anything with a number—.22 caliber, .25, .357, .38, .45, .50, .410, 10 gauge, 12, 16—was there one second, then gone the next. Ammunition remained on the shelves, but there was nothing to load it into. Bankston screamed, then joined thousands of Americans in calling the police. There would have been millions, but the magnitude of the event had not yet taken hold.*

---

*In Las Cruces, N.M., patrolman Uresti "Sonny" Garza was one of the lucky officers not near a telephone. He would ponder his fortune more this day. He had just pulled over a Honda Civic on the Interstate 10 service road. Garza was surprised when the motorist jumped from the vehicle and began to run. He was even more surprised when he reached for his service* pistol and found nothing there. He reached for his Taser and gave pursuit. After about a quarter mile, the suspect began to tire, putting him in range of Garza's Taser. The juiced needles hit the man in the back, and he crumpled to the ground in a fetal pose. As Garza placed cuffs on the man's hands, the suspect spit at him. "You're lucky I couldn't find my Glock, you pig." Garza squeezed the cuffs tighter. Yeah. Lucky. That's it, he thought.

---

In Cleveland, Jumpy Williams and his cousin, Isaiah Rowlett, were nervously casing out a convenience store from the soft drink section. They had waited for the customers to leave. "Let's go," said Williams, reaching into his jacket pocket and finding ... nothing. "You got your piece?" he asked his cousin. "Where's yo' piece, bro?" Jumpy's jaw dropped, and he shook his head. Isaiah then grabbed for his .32 but discovered that he, too, was unarmed. They looked at one another in bewilderment. As a curious clerk watched, the pair left the store, sullen and confused.

---

A bone-chilled Brian Jacobsson entered the back door of his home in Chisholm, Minn., and he silently moved into the living room. He paused to let the fireplace defuse the cold and remind him of the task at hand. He had read Bitsy's text messages and emails. Today was the day when Chad would come over, when they both thought he was at work. Jacobsson moved down the hallway to the master bedroom. He could hear rustling and moaning coming from his ... what, sanctuary? Then he heard Bitsy cooing. "That's it. That's it. Right there. Unhh. UNHH ... ohhh." Jacobsson moved into the room; Bitsy screamed. Chad covered himself with a pillow. Goodbye, Bitsy. Goodbye, Chad. That pillow won't stop a bullet, he thought as he reached into his coat for his father's Vietnam War .45 he taken from his desk. But it wasn't there. Momentarily taken aback, Jacobsson began to laugh. "What the everloving hell?" he shouted at the ceiling as the two naked people before him leapt from the bed and scrambled for whatever semblance of havens they could find. "Fuck you, Bitsy. Fuck you, Chad." Jacobsson laughed again and aimed finger pistols at each of them. Then he began to sob.

# CHAPTER 34

*A larger group of men were deep within a forest that day, this one in Idaho, but they weren't looking for deer. The camo-clad gaggle—an offshoot of the Boogaloo Boys—had just received a batch of kits to convert their AR-15s to full auto, and now it was time to test them out. Targets of various kinds had been nailed to trees. Some of the targets had been spray-painted "FBI" or "ATF." Chaz Wertzknopf went to his van, bedecked with sticker slogans like "Live Free or You Die," "Guns Don't Kill But We Do" and "Only Amendment Two Matters", to retrieve the new cache of weapons. He opened the rear doors ... and found only air.*

*Sylvia Dershwood locked her bedroom door and sat on the edge of her bed. The pimply-faced sixteen-year-old in Orangeburg, South Carolina, felt the tears make slow rivulets down her face. She held a note in her hand, a response note from a boy she thought was friendly, maybe even sweet on her. She had passed him a note in geography class to catch his attention. But this boy's head had been turned all right—although not by her. She knew who her competition was. Go to hell, Brittany, she thought. You little whore. Sylvia erupted with a primal cry of emotion, weeping until she could cry no more. She opened her nightstand drawer and reached for her father's pistol. She had hidden the gun inside the drawer days before, burying it under headbands, faded Valentines, and a jumble of Swiftie bracelets, just for a moment like this. Sylvia moved her hand all around the drawer. Finding nothing, she pulled out the drawer and turned it upside down. She scattered the pile for a better look. Daddy's pistol wasn't there.*

*Joey Bernard was stuck up in a tree deep in the Piney Woods of East Texas. The twelve-year-old was on his second deer hunting trip, but it was the first time he was on his own. His father, uncle, and grandfather were ensconced in their own deer blind about seventy yards away with Jim Beam keeping them warm. The men had left the pre-teen boy alone in winter's grasp to "toughen him up" and "become a man." The bone-chilled boy shivered as the wind moved the leaves about him; he passed the time by using his buck knife to carve "Joey + Allie" into one of deer stand boards. As he put away the knife, he became wide-eyed at the sight of an eight-point buck that had just sauntered imperiously from the wood and now was within range. He raised his rifle, feeling its heft. But in an instant, there was no longer a rifle there. No telescopic sight, no strap, no trigger. Joey was holding ... nothing. Say what?!?, he shouted. The deer pounced away.*

---

*Down south in the Lone Star State, along the Rio Grande outside of Eagle Pass, three members of the Texas Border Volunteers squatted in the reeds along the shoreline watching a group of twenty to twenty five migrants approach the river. The men had parked their $125,000 Hummer SUV a quarter mile away from their observation perch. The migrants were a mixed bag of a few men, but mostly women and children. Two of the camo-clad Volunteers carried 9 mm handguns with extended clips, but the third had a new XM556 handheld machine gun, a mini Gatling gun capable of firing 1,300 rounds in ten seconds. They remained silent and under cover as the group approached the river. From what they could overhear, the group leader or guide was named Ernesto. What the three Volunteers didn't know is that Ernesto had led the core of the group—a few others joined along the way—all the way from Guatemala, in flight from drug gangs trying to recruit child sicarios. Ernesto was using a five-foot walking stick to test the depth of the river, and when he got about halfway across, he signaled the rest forward. The Volunteers readied their weapons but remained silent. Ernesto came ashore, produced some wire cutters and began clearing a path through the razor wire. Once the entire group was ensconced on the Texas side of the Rio Grande, the trio rose. One of them shouted, "You shitbags hold it right there!" Ernesto and the others raised their hands—but dropped them in shock when they saw the weapons carried by their accosters ... simply vanish. The three Volunteers looked at one another in stunned disbelief. Ernesto shouted, "Get them. Get them now." The adult migrants grabbed sticks, bottles, and rocks and began bombarding the trio of Volunteers, striking one. The other two ran. Ernesto carefully wrapped a strand of*

## CHAPTER 34

*razor wire around one end of his walking stick and approached the fallen Volunteer. He raised the stick above his head. "Who's a shitbag now, gringo?" were the final words the Volunteer heard.*

---

*There were certainly no bucks inside the Walmart in Hernando, but the gun counter where Terry Clyde Tolliver had bought his murder weapon just a few weeks before was busy just the same. In fact, in some circles, the gun counter was kind of a local shrine. Bo Schwamkrag, a Walmart customer this day, was thinking Tolliver should have taken out some old Jews instead of shooting up the Waffle Barn. The bacon there was not half bad, he thought. Well, Bo thought to himself, I don't know if any Jews are about, but I do know there is an Islamic Center over in Starkville. Somebody ought to pay them ragheads a visit. Bo called the clerk over and said, "Let me look at that one," pointing to an AR-15 in a glass case. "Sure thing," said the clerk, who took out a key and opened the case. As the glass slid to the side, the AR-15 disappeared. Along with every other gun in store. Bo and the clerk looked at one another. "WHAT THE FUCK?" they said.*

---

Multiply these stories by millions and that was what America had become. Gun manufacturers continued to churn but only as an act of vanity. Museum curators were left with empty exhibits. Fear became the national drink. Rising numbers of Americans sought the protection of churches, temples, and mosques. On the other hand, some Canadians told reporters that now might be a good time to travel to America again.

Meanwhile, the hunt for the mysterious Radley Duvall was placed on a back burner. For now, America, exhaling a collective anguish while hiding behind its walls of paranoia, only wanted to know: Where are the guns?

## CHAPTER 35

That was the primary question before an emergency Cabinet session called the next morning. The president wanted to meet earlier, but the breadth of the "event" had left the nation in shocked paralysis. The White House also wanted to include each of the states' governors and the D.C. mayor in the meeting via remote, no small feat to arrange.

The president called the meeting to order. "I need an update on the situation. So, who wants to go first?"

The secretary of Homeland Security raised his hand. "Here's what we know at present, Mr. President. It appears that all firearms in possession by U.S. civilians have suddenly vanished and without explanation. This disappearance includes all ranges of weapons—from handguns to long guns of all types, meaning shotguns and rifles. Additionally, as far as we can determine, all law enforcement agencies have been similarly impacted. Any business that sells guns was also affected.

"At this moment, Mr. President, we have no idea where these weapons have gone," he continued. "That anomaly overlaps with the investigation portion of the agenda, which will be covered by the FBI director."

# CHAPTER 35

"Anomaly," repeated the president. "Let's not use that word with our friends on the right. They see this as either an apocalypse or the Second Coming."

The White House chief of staff chimed in. "I'm thinking we can describe this as only a 'crisis' for now, Mr. President, since the nation is not in any eminent danger."

The president turned to the chairman of the Joint Chiefs of Staff. "Can you elaborate on that?"

"Mr. President, for reasons we cannot explain ..."

"There's a lot of that going around," inserted the president. "Go on."

"Yes, sir. For reasons we cannot explain at the present time, all branches of the military remain armed except for National Guard units. They are in the same boat as the civilian population. To clarify, when I say all other branches remain armed, that includes hand weapons, artillery, armor, aircraft, naval vessels ... all the way up to ICBMs. All of our nuclear and chemical weapons systems appear to be in working order, sir."

The president paused, wiping his eyeglass lenses with his handkerchief. Then he looked about the room. "So, what do we know about this Radley Duvall character?"

"You mean, Boo, sir?" chuckled the FBI director. "I can't believe Cowley fell for that. Then again, yes, I can. Boo Radley was a central character in 'To Kill a Mockingbird.' It was Robert Duvall's first film role if I recall correctly. Radley and Duvall. Radley Duvall. In any event, we haven't been able to find a lawyer or anyone else by that name. We are still checking databases."

"Uh-huh. Why am I not surprised," said the president. "Do we have any idea how this was done? Who has the technology to pull this off?"

The CIA director and the Pentagon chief looked at one another. The former said, "Sir, as far as we know, this technology doesn't exist. But obviously it does. I'm not one to ascribe this event to being of a religious nature. From examination of the hearing room video, we can see that Mr. Duvall does something with his watch at the same time he makes his declaration. We don't know if there is a connection."

The general concurred, "I don't believe in miracles either. But whatever did this, boy, that would be lovely to have on our side."

"Thank you, gentlemen. Yes, I can well imagine that Moscow and Beijing would also love to get their hands on this technology, wherever it came from. What is our threat level at. Anything on the proverbial radar screen?" asked the president.

"We have raised the overall threat level to DefCon 2, which is something we often do in a situation … uh, crisis … such as this one," the chairman replied. "There global situation remains much the same as it did a few days ago. The conflicts in Eastern Europe and the Middle East are ongoing, but there is nothing new among our adversaries except an increase in message traffic." The chairman looked toward the director of the National Security Agency, who nodded his concurrence.

The general continued, "We think the messaging from the White House and cooperation of the news media has helped to keep the bad guys at bay. Of course, we have been inundated with messages seeking assurance from our allies in NATO, SEATO, and elsewhere, and we have been quick to comply."

The secretary of State chimed in at this point. "Our department has been assisting with calming the friendlies as well, Mr. President. So far, everyone seems to be placated, except for the usual suspects, France and Israel. We will have to do some additional handholding with them."

"What are their concerns?"

"What you would expect. Can we honor our defense obligations. Can we fulfill our arms deals," said the secretary of Defense.

"Hmmm. Well, thank you, general. Thank you, Mr. Secretary. Anything else before we move on?" asked the president.

Both men nodded in the negative. "OK, what are we looking at domestically?"

The attorney general spoke up. "My department is going to need some assistance handling the flood of phone calls from state and municipal police agencies," he said. "Understandably, they are in

# CHAPTER 35

panic mode, and it doesn't help when they get put on hold. Which we have no choice but to do at the moment. Perhaps a presidential address can alleviate that? In the meantime, any and all help will be appreciated. If I'm not mistaken, I believe Homeland Security is getting swamped as well." The Homeland Security secretary mouthed a "thank you" to the attorney general.

The White House press secretary spoke up. "The president will be making an address to the nation tonight in prime time. In the interim, and for the foreseeable future, we will be sending out advisories and updates every two hours. We are in the process of creating a separate 800 number for law enforcement agencies to contact with inquiries. The vice president and her staff have agreed to oversee domestic law enforcement concerns during this crisis."

Taking her cue, the vice president said, "The number one question we are hearing is whether the military can furnish weapons to the police agencies. I don't think there is a protocol for that. This administration has furnished many types of equipment through the various 'War on Drugs' programs, but not weapons."

"That is something the Department of Justice is looking into, Mr. President," said the attorney general. "But our initial determination is that congressional action would be required first. It's all very preliminary, however."

The president nodded, pursed his lips and perused through some of the documents before him. "What about domestic incidents?"

"We haven't received reports a single shooting anywhere in the country for the past … (looking at her watch) … twenty-four hours, Mr. President," said the head of the White House Office on Gun Violence, a relatively new agency. "Typically, we see hundreds of shootings daily and more than a hundred fatalities. It's rather remarkable, really."

"Yes, remarkable. But what has been the public reaction?"

The Homeland Security chief said, "Most people appear to be hunkering down, trying to figure out what's going on. Like we are. I have a few incidents to report, only because they might escalate. We received a report that militia groups in Idaho and Montana have stormed gun stores looking for weapons. There has been some property damage and subsequent arrests, but no serious injuries."

The president interrupted. "How are police securing these arrests?"

"With Tasers and batons, sir. And numbers," said the secretary. "Out in San Francisco this morning, a man later identified as a homeless meth head tried to rob a bank by using his finger. He wasn't successful. We have also seen scattered news reports of demonstrations by gun control groups in support of ... whatever this is. They have been fervent but peaceful. No reported clashes with pro-gun groups. Moms Against Guns, survivors of the Stoneman Douglas High School slaughter, and the Sandy Hook parents have all issued statements. And on the flip side, so has the NRA, although I must say, its statement resembles something you might find on an Alex Jones conspiracy program."

Homeland's border protection chief raised his hand. "We are also seeing news reports of traffic gridlock on both our southern and northern borders, presumably by folks trying to buy firearms in Canada and Mexico. For once it appears we have more people trying to get into Mexico than vice versa."

The governor of Nevada signaled in from among the remote audience. "Mr. President, let me second what the border chief just said. Is there any way we can get assistance to check vehicles coming back from Mexico? I'm guessing the governors of Michigan and New York might be wanting the same for travelers from Canada."

"Let me address this to all of the governors who joined this feed. First, deploy your National Guard personnel ... they still have batons and tear gas, right? ... as you see fit. But make sure that any and all military armories located in your states are protected. We don't need any of the swastika crowd or any gangs stealing military weapons," said the president. "Let's see how things play out over the next few days before authorizing the military to act. No sense invoking the Insurrection Act if we don't have to."

The governor of Texas saw an opening. "Mr. President, what is the federal government doing to catch the pond scum behind all

# CHAPTER 35

this? Seems to me we could get a lot of answers by sweating him in a West Texas jail. Do we know if he's an Antifa agent?"

The president pointed at the FBI director. "Your turn."

"Mr. President, right now, we have no idea of this Radley Duvall is a member of Antifa, the Proud Boys, or any group, for that matter," said the director, chomping on his ever present but unlit pipe. "As I said in our earlier briefing, we can find no documentary evidence of the existence of anyone by that name. The Justice Department is subpoenaing photo images from the news media to match his picture to available databases using facial recognition."

He continued, "At present, we have no evidence indicating how he got into the Capitol. We are not getting much from security cameras inside or outside the building. Capitol Police have no record of him going through security."

Indignant, the Texas governor snarled, "So, what are you fed boys doing besides shining shoes and sitting on your collective arses?"

"We do have a few leads that we are following up on, sir," said the FBI director. "That's all I am at liberty to say for now."

Seeing partisan cracks starting to form, the president delivered a verbal gavel. "Alright now, let's keep our tempers on a leash. We are all swimming in a pool of gray, so let's try to get some answers. We will meet again tomorrow at the same time. Thank you all."

## CHAPTER 36

Radley Duvall would never be found. Like the guns, he had disappeared, or at least faded into nothingness within the device on Anton's wrist. It was Roy McDonald who returned to Memphis and then to Eudora and then to the warm embrace of Ellie Atkinson.

First things first. He found Jonnie Barnes in the RV park manager's office and paid him for his caretaker duties. He then took an Uber to Hernando.

"Can you believe what just happened? There are no guns anywhere. No more school shootings. My kids will be safe," she said, pummeling Roy with her excitement. "And you were there when it happened. What was it like?"

"I wasn't quite there, but I guess I was close enough. There were cops all over the place. It took me forever to get through airport security," he replied. "But things were pretty boring where I was. Same city, but we were across town. Just climate change, climate change, climate change. No carbon emissions disappeared, too, did they?"

She laughed. "Not that I know of. Anyway, people are just freaking out. The school board has been talking about closing schools. But here's the funny thing about that."

## CHAPTER 36

"What's that?" Roy asked.

"They said on the news tonight that nobody in America has been shot in two days. *Two days*. Why close schools when there's no danger? It's too bad this didn't happen a few months ago," she said, conjuring a memory of Ezra.

"No one shot in two days. Wow. I wonder how long it's been since that happened. Maybe before the Pilgrims," Roy surmised. He reached into a small plastic bag and handed the contents to Ellie. "I got you a little something. It's a Lincoln Memorial snow globe. Might make a great paperweight on your desk, Miss Atkinson."

"Thank you so much. That's so considerate," she said, showing her gratitude with a kiss. Gator hopped up and down on Roy's leg. "This little guy missed you, too."

Roy scratched the tiny dog's head and ears. "I'm so beat. All I want to do is sit with you and Gator."

"I think we can arrange that," she said.

## CHAPTER 37

Sub-Protector Korphan fell back in his chair as the unsettling reports from field operatives filtered into the Xylodonian Protectorate. A prominent nation on Earth had undergone a seismic change, an alteration that had occurred within seconds—most of that nation's hand weapons had vanished. There was a remarkable consistency to those weapons that did not disappear.

Such an event could only have been achieved through Xylodonian technology, and there was only one Xylodonian operative who was unaccounted for—Anton. Well, except for the one who died mysteriously. The body was never found. So tragic for her family.

The gun disappearance, coupled with the Memphis incident that also bore Xylodonian earmarks, had pushed Korphan far past forgiveness. The future of Xylodon was literally at stake, some of his colleagues told him. Decades of silent observation and the subsequent knowledge feed were being jeopardized and immediate action was needed, they said. A good number of Korphan's colleagues added that these acts, if proven to have been conducted by a Xylodon Guardian, could be considered treasonous and perhaps deserving of the ultimate punishment.

# CHAPTER 37

After overcoming various delays, a craft had finally been dispatched to bring new companions to join or relieve Anton. Now, Korphan decided, the mission had to change. New orders were prepared.

Korphan sent an encrypted message to those on the vessel, which was still a considerable distance from Earth. One problem—the two-person crew was skilled but not very experienced. This was an unprecedented situation. He had to make sure the message was firm.

"Once you get him on board, arrest Anton-7."

"Acknowledged. What is the procedure after he is informed of his arrest?" was the reply.

"You are free to do as circumstances dictate. Bind him. Sedate him. Your decision. There should be a holding area you can keep him in."

"Acknowledged. And what if he resists?"

"You are authorized to use lethal force if necessary. Kill him."

After a pause ... "Acknowledged."

## CHAPTER 38

Over the next few weeks, America fell into an uneasy calm. Even the news networks had dropped the gun disappearance story from the lead position. Pro-gun acolytes continued to wail but seemed to be treading water in the face of what was—or was not—occurring. Gun control advocates clucked their "I-told-you-so's," noting that the nation was still adequately shielded by its military. They promoted this moment as not only abiding by the original meaning of the Second Amendment but as a second chance for the nation.

Twenty-nine days had lapsed since the last time a gun had claimed a life in the United States, although some shootings had occurred as attempts to stem gun flow at the borders were not entirely successful. About a dozen people were wounded in various confrontations across the borders, many of them looting-related incidents. Some of the incidents were born from conspiracy theories that suggested that "Illuminati agents" had engaged in mass confiscation. In any case, it was far from the daily death toll the nation had tucked away under thoughts and prayers.

The truth of the matter was the guns were not gone. Well, not gone-gone. They were moved. Into another dimension of sorts.

# CHAPTER 38

Millions of guns could no longer be seen, no longer be touched, no longer be fired. They were now in the "cold, dead hands" of a plane of existence far beyond the reach of humans. America had been made the victim of a massive parlor trick, a delusion of illusion. It was a variation on one form of banishment widely used by the Xylodonian judiciary decades before. Anton had interfaced one of the features of his watch—one that broke down matter into its component parts for instant transfer to a designated area. Some called it the "particle disseminator" effect. The resulting signal emission was a boon to Xylodonian builders, the beam could be used for lifting or removing heavy objects. Members of the Xylodonian security forces had learned that this feature could have offensive or defensive capabilities as well—there was no requirement to reconstitute the atoms or molecules that had been collected. Gone was gone.

The beam could be boosted, but controlled, using the array atop Anton's RV. Creating the beam was but step one; it had to programmed upon what to feed. It had taken Anton hours upon hours to scan in the image of every Earth firearm into his computer database so that the beam emitted would recognize every derringer, every BB gun, every assault rifle. But Anton wasn't content with having his "gun snatcher" simply recognize shapes—he programmed the transmission to recognize the molecules unique to gun metal. That turned out to be no easy feat—there was a variation in the metals used. Procuring test "subjects" wasn't easy either, despite Mississippi's loose gun laws. Anton had to use different human forms to purchase a dozen or so pistols and rifles. Anton was extremely pleased with himself after the initial test applications were successful. Any guns that were "touched" by the beam or entered the beam's perimeter—he both placed or tossed the procured guns into the beam's path—were dispatched to the assigned dimension. *Zeesnaarst!* he thought. Success!

But Anton's work was far from done. He now had to designate the "shielded zones" for his beam; he accomplished this by accessing Xylodonian Security Forces computer files that gave the locations and profiles of every mainland American military base. The sophisticated Xylodonian technology was also able to map, via vast global positioning data, the outline of the entire United States, including Alaska and Hawaii. That process wasn't as difficult as the gun-scanning operation, and including the American territories of Guam and Puerto Rico was a bit tricky. There were other complications—what to do about the National Guard units located in the various states? Those facilities were not part of the Xylodonian database. Anton attempted to pinpoint the National Guard sites, but there were just too many of them and the data too imprecise. The Guardsmen would just have to suffer the same fate as their countrymen.

After the last data entry, Anton paused to take a break. He poured himself some iced tea and turned on the television, immediately beginning to channel-surf. When he got to Channel 387, he stopped. His face turned white. "What the …?" he said aloud. On the screen was a program about new inventions, and this one was highlighting 3D printers. Somehow, fate had caused him to land on this television program at the exact moment 3-D guns were being produced by the printer. The program host explained that these plastic-based items were being called "ghost guns" and were virtually undetectable by security devices designed to detect metallic guns.

*Girgach!* These "ghost guns" were a factor he hadn't expected; they threatened to throw a huge plastic monkey wrench into Anton's plan. How widespread were these printers? He flipped off the television and went to his computer; a quick search stunned and sickened him. They were everywhere. There were even 3-D printers being made for kids these days—just $229 plus shipping from one website. What good would it do to make metallic guns disappear if these American humans could just make new ones out of plastic?

Google came to the rescue—along with J.D. Williams, whoever he was. Mississippi was far from being overrun by 3-D printers, and he had little time to order one. Anton learned that the closest device was at the University of Mississippi over in Oxford; it had a 3D printer in its J.D. Williams Library available to all students and faculty. *All praise to modern education,* Anton thought. It would be a six-hour plus drive back and forth, maybe longer on his scooter, but Anton knew it had to be done if his plan had any chance to succeed. He left early the next morning and got to the campus before 10 a.m.

## CHAPTER 38

The drive and finding visitor parking turned out to be the hardest parts of this endeavor.

He found the library easily enough and then located the 3-D printer. His "Roy the botanist" form blended in well with the assorted cast members of academia. He had to wait as a short line of students used the printer to fulfill some class requirement or some wanton desire. The student just before him created what appeared to be a very life-like, nine-inch dildo. *Of course he did*, Anton thought. *What else would higher learning be for? I'm guessing that's not for class, but who am I to judge?*

After Mr. Dildo sauntered away—*where is he going to hide that?*—it was Anton's turn. He wasn't so much interested in creating something as he was in the material used in the creative process. Still, while he was here … so, he programmed the machine after scanning in a photo of little Gator, and within a few minutes he had a plastic replica of his favorite furry four-footed friend. Since he was not going to keep this one, he made another as a gift for Ellie. He pocketed the two plastic chiweenies and headed back to Eudora.

By early afternoon, he was updating the recognition sequences on his beam apparatus to include the 3-D printer material. The molecules were easily read into the system. Now, came the first test.

Anton initialized the system, and the array began to hum. He focused the beam on a stump behind the RV, just as he had in his gun metal tests. After ascertaining that there were no unwanted eyes on his activities, Anton tossed one of the plastic Gators toward the stump.

It disappeared.

*Zeesnaarst! It works!*

## CHAPTER 39

The federal government continued to monitor the "crisis" and send out soothing messages to the public and overseas allies. But there were disturbing reports as well—authorities observed a significant rise in online gun purchases from overseas websites, although the packages appeared empty on arrival. Additionally, local police saw a rise in home break-ins by gangs no longer afraid of being shot by the occupants. That advent gave rise to increased security system sales. Protests by far-right groups espousing a variety of conspiracy theories increased in state capitals and in Washington. Some fringe television pundits called upon Russia to send weaponry to America.

There were other collateral effects. The National Rifle Association saw donations and membership begin to drop. Some states that had apportioned funds for school security—Texas, for instance, had recently allotted $1.1 billion—began to wonder if those monies could be better used elsewhere.

Even as the nation struggled with its new normal, federal authorities continued to seek out the person believed to be responsible. If "Radley Duvall" could flip a switch and take the guns away, then he could flip a switch and bring them back—or so the thinking went.

# CHAPTER 39

The FBI director shared the progress of the agency's investigation at the next presidential Cabinet briefing. The director presented an array of still images to reflect when agents had uncovered.

"Through our analysis of security camera footage, we have found some unusual occurrences that may be pointing us in a promising direction. Photo one was taken by an outdoor Capitol security camera and shows a young African American boy carrying a briefcase. This was the same boy encountered by Capitol police officers in a restroom moments after Duvall left the House hearing room. Photos two and three are blowups of the briefcase. You will note the similarities. Plus, how often do you see ten-year-olds with briefcases instead of backpacks?"

The president interjected. "Are you suggesting the boy is our perpetrator?"

"No, Mr. President. But he may be an accomplice or provide us information about Duvall," said the director. "The next series of photos you see were taken by various cameras along the Washington Mall. They show the boy, still carrying the briefcase, entering the Capitol South Metrorail station at about 3:22 p.m.

"These next images were taken within the Capitol South station. Look closely at the video ... the boy goes into a restroom with the briefcase, but a Caucasian male leaves the restroom carrying what appears to be the same briefcase. We went through another twelve hours of security footage and never saw the boy emerge from the restroom. Those restrooms are cleaned at regular intervals. There have been no reports of foul play. So, where did the boy go? That's another mystery wrapped within this enigma.

"The man is shown getting on the train and later disembarking at a Metrorail substation outside the city. It took us some time to find the right substation, and then we got lucky. As you can see in Photo eight, for some reason he looked directly at the camera before walking away. Our agents took blowups of that photo to various hotels in that area, and we got lucky again. A Hilton Garden Inn desk manager recognized the man as being a recent guest. That guest was identified as a Roy McDonald.

"But that only brings us to another mystery. Roy McDonald.

Records indicate he's from Cromwell, Connecticut, but there is no one by that name at the address given. It appears he spent some time in New Hampshire as well. He was supposedly educated at Yale, but Yale has no records on him. He doesn't appear to have a Social Security number either. So, who is he? We don't know.

"What we do know," the director continued, "is that he boarded a plane in Memphis to come to Washington, and he flew back to Memphis after leaving Washington. We have agents on the ground now in Memphis trying to determine where he went after he landed."

"Outstanding work, Mr. Director," said the president. "So, this Roy McDonald is your prime suspect?"

"He certainly is a person of interest, Mr. President. We'll determine if he's a suspect once we find him and bring him in for questioning."

"Thank you, Mr. Director. Please keep us apprised. Anything else? No? OK, I think we can adjourn for now."

By the time the meeting ended, America had marked its thirtieth consecutive day without a gun fatality.

## CHAPTER 40

The sun was bright, but it was still cold in Brussels, the headquarters of the European Union. The ministers from Sweden, Germany, and France were ensconced in an anteroom tending to their tea and coffee. A plate bearing a variety of Danishes sat untouched.

The French minister looked up from the latest edition of Le Monde. "Did you see this story? The Americans have gone nearly a month without anyone being killed by a firearm. It's really quite *stupéfiante*. It's been a long time since one of our countries had more gun deaths than the Americans. It is no longer the America we thought we knew. The one where the Statue of Liberty carries a rifle instead of a torch."

"Yes," said the German minister. "And what's more amazing, their FBI and CIA have not been able to determine how all the guns disappeared. That's four hundred million guns and not a single clue as to where they are. But whatever did it, *mein gott*, wouldn't it be grand to have that technology."

"I bet our friends in Moscow and Beijing are a bit nervous these days," said the Frenchman.

"Not to mention our friends in Tehran and Pyongyang," added

the Swede. "I must say, though, that some of the protests out in America's cowboy lands are a bit worrisome. You would think they would be content with having more than five thousand nuclear warheads."

"Indeed," said the German. "But how does one carry a nuclear warhead while cosplaying as Rambo?"

The three men chortled.

The Frenchman pointed at the newspaper. "This article goes on to say that some American news broadcasters on the right-wing networks are actually calling on the Russians to send weapons to the United States. They think that reminding Boris of all the assistance America gave Uncle Joe during World War II will lead to reciprocation. Can you imagine? The inmates are truly screaming at the asylum doors these days in the U S of A."

The German nodded. "I'm sure you saw the reports from our former member to the north about the Irish freighter caught by the American Navy carrying weapons to Boston. A few decades ago, it was the other way around. Now, Ireland is supplying America. Or trying to."

The Swede poured himself some more coffee and sampled one of the Danishes. After swallowing, he noted, "Well, these unexpected events have been a boon to our economies. More Europeans are unafraid to visit the Disney parks these days."

"Here, here," said the German, raising his cup. "All power to the Mouse!"

## CHAPTER 41

The failure of various gun-smuggling attempts did not deter others from trying. But in each case, Anton's improvised "gun shield" proved up to the task. The eyes of Americans seeking guns turned northward, finding a good number of Canadian friends willing to oblige—for a profit. However, no matter the mode of transportation—truck, train, or plane—each endeavor from the Great North met with the same stunning fate: once the vehicle reached American soil the weapons would disappear. These outcomes were mostly known only to the smugglers and "smug-glees;" U.S. authorities were only able to thwart a few of these operations beforehand.

A similar venture from China fared no better. A ship bearing two cargo containers filled with AK-47s and various handguns docked in Los Angeles and unloaded its contraband, masked by dozens of other containers. The smugglers entered the facility surreptitiously in the night and located their two targets. But, again, once opened they were as empty as a politician's promises.

Still, this lack of success—with no small expenditure of funds—only served to ignite the ingenuity of the smugglers.

Ernesto, the human smuggler who had helped chase off the three members of the Texas Border Volunteers, had turned his attention to another part of the Texas border. In an area just outside the labyrinth of Juarez, Mexico, a city fueled by clandestine deals, there existed a dilapidated warehouse. Within its crumbling facade a modern-day operation thrived in the underbelly of the city. This was the nerve center of a sophisticated smuggling syndicate, where goods—mostly humans and drugs—flowed like dark currents beneath the surface. But now there was another, more deadly, commodity being sought by the gringos—guns. Ernesto was only too happy to try to make a buck—thousands of them in this case—from the gun lust.

Mexico itself has only one gun store in the entire nation—the Directorate of Arms and Munitions Sales—which is operated by the army and located on a military base. Those seeking a firearm must provide six documents and wait months to receive their prize. About 70 percent of the weapons seized by Mexican authorities annually originate with legal gun dealers in the United States and were smuggled across the border. Ernesto chuckled at the irony of forcing the gringos to pay for their own guns.

At the heart of his venture lay a tunnel—a passage carved deep into the earth, connecting the warehouse to a nondescript storage unit across the border in El Paso. It was constructed with meticulous precision—a feat born of desperation and necessity in equal measure. Its walls were lined with reinforced steel and food, water, and medical supplies were concealed behind false panels. The tunnel, about ten yards down and several hundred yards long, was lighted across its entire length and was somewhat cooled by a crude attempt at air conditioning via holes drilled in PVC pipes. A man of average height could walk upright with ease.

The tunnel operation had subsisted in secret for nearly a decade, but it was not without peril. American authorities had learned of the tunnel's existence but were unable to pinpoint where it emerged. But the attention of the gringos—and the increased bribes demanded by Mexican lawmen—caused the tunnel to be shut down. But the events in the north provided a strong allure. For Ernesto and the others in the know, the tunnel was a beacon of opportunity. If there was one thing that Mexico's underground had access to, it was guns.

# CHAPTER 41

The warehouse that cloaked one tunnel entrance was a fortress of secrecy, guarded by loyal lieutenants who kept watchful eyes on the comings and goings of all who dared to approach. There were similar safeguards taken at what was primarily the exit, hidden with a secluded unit within the El Paso storage facility. There were connecting units that were never leased that could be used as needed. The legal operations of the storage company turned a small profit, which was another plus and added to the deception.

Ernesto was put in charge of an initial shipment—twenty boxes holding an assortment of assault rifles and handguns, plus a few shotguns—as part of a test run. "The gringos have plenty of ammunition already. They just need our guns," Ernesto told his crew. Using his own funds, Ernesto arranged for metal wheeled gurneys to carry the boxes to the Texas side, and he had paid for small pneumatic lifts on both ends of the tunnel to speed the cargo along.

The first part of the operation was easily carried out; the twenty boxes were lowered into the tunnel and placed on the gurneys. The heavier rifle boxes were placed one to a single gurney, while the smaller handgun boxes could be doubled up. Ernesto, taking every precaution, had his crew spray the gurney wheel bearing with lubricant to reduce any sounds during the traverse. He ordered his men and their respective loads to keep twenty feet apart, again to reduce a concentration of sound. Ernesto then grabbed a bottle of water and a cigar and trudged down the tunnel and into El Paso to help with the extraction.

Pushing the gurneys down the tunnel occurred without event; as the contraband-laden train made its way forward, a gurney bearing a box of rifles was the first to arrive below the storage unit. Two men were needed to load the box onto the lift. A red button was pushed, and the box was hoisted upward toward the opening. One of Ernesto's men reached for a rope handle—and found that the box easily slid from the lift to the concrete floor. "I think something is wrong, *el jefe*," said the man.

"What is it?"

"The box is too light."

"Open it up."

The accomplice used a small crowbar to crack open the box. It was empty.

"*Hijo de puta!*" shouted Ernesto, who peered into the tunnel. "This box is empty. What did you two *cabrons* do?"

"Nothing, *jefe*. I swear," said the man operating the lift.

"Open up the next box and send it up," Ernesto commanded.

The two men who had sent up the first box did as they were ordered, removing the box top and sending up a crate of AK-47s. Ernesto watched the operation intently. But once the box reached the surface—technically U.S. soil—the weapons disappeared.

"*La puta madre!*" screamed Ernesto, turning to his companions. "Did you see that?"

"Yes, *jefe*. This is the devil's work."

Ernesto addressed the pair still in the tunnel as the other gurneys arrived. "This time just send up one pistol."

A box was opened, a pistol found and lifted above. The same result was witnessed. Now you see it, now you don't.

"*Chingao*. This can't be happening," Ernesto shouted. He paused and walked away from the opening, lighting his cigar as he thought. He returned to his stunned crew.

"All right let's send everything back. We won't get the same price that we would in Houston or Dallas, but we maybe we can put something in our pockets," he told the men.

*It was a lot easier smuggling Venezuelans,* Ernesto thought. *Venezuelans don't disappear.*

## CHAPTER 42

Ernesto was far from the only one experiencing frustration. Derek Bankston, the Iowa gun shop operator, was also feeling the same churn in his stomach. Still, he came to his store each day ... hoping, just as thousands of other gun store owners likely did. *My family still has to eat*, he thought.

Bankston was able to scrape his survival together by selling knives and chemical agents, such as pepper spray, Mace, and bear repellent. Just as with long guns, the bigger the knife the better. He would run out of Bowie knives as soon as they came in. There appeared to be a growing interest in tactical armor.

A recent radio report offered a possible explanation for that—and gave him an idea. The nation's hardware stores were experiencing a frenzied run on machetes, scythes, and similar tools. The few U.S. sword manufacturers had become inundated with purchases, and soon the back orders turned into months. Bankston was unable to get through to the sword companies, but he did manage to secure a machete shipment.

*Americans were anything if not creative when it came to defending themselves and their property*, he thought, smiling as he pictured a modern-day "Game of Thrones" with horseback riders in tactical gear dueling with swords and knives.

Had he known, he might have ordered up some Louisville sluggers as well—sporting goods stores across the country were unable to keep bats and hockey sticks on their shelves. The sudden windfall bled over into alarm manufacturers as well, and more than a few former gun store employees saw their desperation turn them into alarm installers.

Bankston fired up his computer and checked on the arrival dates of his most recent orders. *At least the shipping industry is still up and running*, he mused. *If I can sell a dozen or so machetes, I can take the family out to dinner and a movie.*

The bell atop the store's front door jingled to life. A Mutt and Jeff duo wearing ballcaps, sunglasses, and thick cotton shirt-jackets entered the store.

"Morning, gents. Can I help you?" said Bankston.

"No thanks. Just looking," said "Mutt," who wandered toward the back.

"Take your time. Nobody here to get in your way."

Bankston's eyes went back to his computer, but he soon looked up when "Jeff" approached the counter.

"What do you have in the way of knives?" Jeff asked.

"What you see is what I have," said Bankston. "No Bowies at the moment, but I'm expecting a shipment next week."

"Any switchblades?"

"Got some right here," said Bankston, ambling over to another case. He placed a selection of switchblades on the glass counter. "I hear some folks are fastening them onto the ends of poles and tool handles to make spears."

"Is that right? Well, I guess a fella has to do what he has to do," said Jeff, who picked up one of the larger switchblades. "How much is this'n here?"

"That is a Microtech Socom Elite. It's carried by the military police. That one sells for four hundred dollars," said Bankston. "Used to be a bit cheaper but demand has pushed the price up."

"That so? Wouldn't be able to come down on that, would ya?"

## CHAPTER 42

"Well, if you were buying in bulk, I guess I could cut you a …"

Before he could finish the sentence, Bankston noticed that Mutt was now behind him. Startled, he tried to turn but then felt an agonizing pain in his back. He then saw a bloody knife in Mutt's hand. His blood. Mutt then struck again. Bankston tried to move away, but now it was Jeff's turn. He plunged the Socom Elite into Bankston's chest. The shop owner fell to the floor, looking up at the lights. He felt his life ebbing away.

Mutt and Jeff grabbed some shop bags and scooping up knives and whatever else they fancied. Bankston's eyes were still blinking in pain when Jeff came over and stood above him, still holding the Socom Elite.

"Like I told ya. A fella has to do what he has to do."

He then slashed one last time.

## CHAPTER 43

Maintaining the ruse was beginning to consume too much power for Anton to control. His neighbors in the RV park kept asking him why the antennas were humming so much now. He told them something about new weather experiments ordered by Washington, putting them off for the time being.

The "uh-oh" moment arrived a few days later. Anton received an encrypted message from a Xylodonian vessel nearing Earth. The Protectorate was ending the mission and recalling him. The rendezvous time was set at a bit over thirty-seven hours from now, weather and other conditions permitting.

*Thirty-seven hours. That's not much time,* he thought. *What do I tell Ellie?*

He decided to say nothing, spending one last night in her bed. Ellie noticed that their lovemaking seemed to have an extra urgency.

"What was up with you last night, tiger?" she asked, smiling that wicked Ellie smile.

"I guess I was hungry after Washington. Or maybe you're too good of a teacher," he said. Her wicked smile became wickeder.

They finished their coffees, and Ellie got work ready. Roy gave

## CHAPTER 43

her a hug. "I will be in and out today, so don't be surprised if I don't answer right away. I will be back tonight."

"Looking forward to it," Ellie said. They kissed and went their separate ways.

Roy watched as she drove away, feeling a sense of longing and loss at the same time.

He hurried back to the RV; there was quite a bit involved in shutting down the station. Following protocol, he threw encryption manuals, vital documents, and some equipment into a smoldering burn barrel behind the vehicle. The groceries and non-essential supplies could remain. There were some personal effects he could bring, but he had to remove most traces of his existence here. He downloaded his research findings onto a couple of thumb drives.

Roy had one last item to attend to, an important one for covering his trail. He set the timer on a small high-heat explosive device that would destroy any remaining evidence inside the RV. The blast would also destroy or severely damage the antenna array atop the RV, meaning the range of his gun disappearance feat would be reduced to little more than the RV park. *Well, it couldn't go on forever,* he thought.

Those efforts took much of the day to complete. The weight of the pending departure clouded his concentration. There was more to do first.

Anton did some weather and cloud cover checks, raising an eyebrow. He then sent a message to the approaching Xylodonian ship, suggesting a more advantageous rendezvous site at about six hours from now. He also recommended the extraction be a grab and go. The ship acknowledged his communication.

Next, he sent a text to Ellie. *How about a pizza from Little Mario's tonight. Extra pepperoni.* She gave a heart emoji in reply. *OK. See you around 7,* he wrote.

He then lay down and took a nap.

## CHAPTER 44

Anton rubbed his eyes and went outside to check the burn barrel. Jonnie Barnes came sauntering over, bearing a couple of beers. He handed the unopened one to "Roy."

"Whatcha got going?" Jonnie asked, watching the smoke waft from the barrel.

Roy took a long swig of the cold liquid. "Thanks. Doing some early spring cleaning. You're just the man I needed to see. And not just for this," he said, raising the can.

"You're welcome. Got more in the fridge if you're interested."

"This hits the spot for now. Tell me, what all do you do around here? You have a regular routine?"

"It's pretty much up to my dad. I do some handyman stuff if he needs it. Like painting and fixing the fence. I also help out the residents if they want. You'd be surprised how many clogged toilets I deal with," Jonnie said, avoiding any mention of his nighttime activities. "Why you want to know?"

"Just see how busy you are is all. If you have time, I have a little chore for you."

"Whatever you need as long as it ain't too illegal," Jonnie said.

"I have to go back to Washington for a bit. Better me than you,

## CHAPTER 44

right? I need you to look over the place. Keep the raccoons away. Use the scooter if you need it. Here's the key."

"You can count on me, Roy. Not a problem. Sounds like pretty easy duty."

"Here's a twenty for now, and I will pay you some more when I get back. Don't know how long they are going to keep me so tell me what I owe you when I get back."

"You betcha. Pretty soon this babysitting money is gonna get me a fancy watch like yours," Jonnie said.

"This little thing?" Roy said, tugging at this sleeve and futzing with the device. "Trust me. It's more trouble than it's worth."

The two chatted some more as they finished their beers. Roy shook Jonnie's hand and said his goodbyes. Jonnie wondered what he could take from the burn barrel.

## CHAPTER 45

It was conveniently dark when Roy got on his scooter for the last time. He heard the familiar start and pointed the scooter toward Hernando on Highway 304. After about five minutes, he pulled off the road. All was quiet; he was a bit early.

A short distance away he could see the flashing neon sign for Little Mario's, providing just a bit of welcome light. It also gave him a pang of hunger. *A sausage and onion pizza sure sounds good right now,* he thought. But too late for that.

He checked his surroundings. Once satisfied, he gave a signal and waited.

He could barely see the bluish white Xylodonian craft hovering behind some nearby evergreens. The ship, almost silent, paused over him and emitted a beam of light.

"Roy" was gone. And seconds later, so was the ship.

Miles down the road, a roar jolted the RV park from its slumber. As heads poked out, they saw that strange government vehicle was on fire.

## CHAPTER 45

Ellie looked at the clock. It was close to seven-thirty.

"I'm getting hungry. What about you, Gator?" she said, rubbing the little dog licking its lips.

Ellie called Roy's phone, but it went to voicemail. At about eight, she tried again. Again, voicemail. Worry began to creep in. Highway 304 was a two-lane road without lights until you got close to Hernando.

She waited about ten minutes more, then grabbed a coat, scooped up Gator and got in the Tesla. Ellie tried calling again as she drove. Same response.

Her headlights barely illuminated the road. Gator whimpered, seeming to sense her panic. She spotted Little Mario's and pulled in. The workers told her they had only made deliveries this evening; no one had stopped by to pick up a pie. And, no, they had not seen or heard anything unusual.

Ellie jumped back in the Tesla and drove slowly with her high beams on. She spotted something over to her left, crossed the median and parked on the side of the road with her headlights focused on a familiar object. It was Roy's scooter, turned on its side.

"ROY! ROY! Where are you? Are you hurt?" she shouted. Ellie used her cellphone flashlight as best she could, shouting as she peered through the foliage and shrubs. "ROY! ROY!" She checked the ground for bloodstains or drag marks. Nothing. "ROY! ROY! IT'S ELLIE. ANSWER ME."

No answer came.

Ellie fell to her knees next to the scooter, her head resting on the seat cushion. Heavy sobs welled within her, the only sounds amid the quiet. She didn't know what to think, what to believe. It made no sense. But her pain was real.

She was torn about contacting the police. If she alerted the authorities, it might threaten whatever secret it was that Roy carried. On the other hand, after the events at the Waffle Barn, there was a chance he might be in real danger. Then there was this: What would Kendall Guthrie tell the world if she didn't report Roy's disappearance?

Ellie pulled out her phone.

## CHAPTER 46

Earlier that day, before Roy and Jonnie shared beers and well before a certain RV erupted in flames, agents with the Memphis office of the FBI had continued to pan for information about Roy McDonald at Memphis International Airport. This assignment had come straight from Washington and wouldn't end until D.C. was satisfied.

The trail which had heated up in the early days of the "crisis," had stopped cold in Memphis. The agents questioned the American Airlines and Transportation Security Administration employees who had been present when Roy had flown to Washington, but they were of little help. Too much time and too many travelers had come and gone since then. Security cameras showed Roy McDonald had carried a small suitcase and the briefcase onto his flight. Checks with taxi services had proved unfruitful. If a friend or relative had picked him up after his return, the agents might be completely stymied in finding out where he went.

But fortune again shined on the FBI. The agent assigned to examining security footage shot in the airport exterior found a man matching Roy's description getting into a vehicle in the Uber pickup zone. The license plate was visible.

# CHAPTER 46

Raisul al-Ghazzawi was eating Cheetos in his Nissan while awaiting his first client call when there was a tap at his window. A well-dressed man was holding an FBI identification card for an Agent David Broadscale against the glass. The agent took off his sunglasses and asked Raisul to step outside.

"What's this about, sir?" Raisul asked.

"On or about January 25 of this year, were you providing Uber services around the Memphis airport?" asked the agent, who then displayed a photo of a man getting into Raisul's Nissan.

"That sounds right. I drive nearly every day to make a living. That looks like my car in the picture."

"Any chance you recognize this man? Know where he was headed?"

"No, can't say as I know him. Did you say it was January 25? Looks like nighttime in the picture. Let me check my phone app," said Raisul. The driver thumbed through his bookings. "This must be it. I only had one client on the night of the twenty-fifth. Oh, yeah, right. He wanted me to drive him to Eudora, Mississippi. First time I'd ever been there. It was a $111 fare. Gave me a nice tip and review."

"Eudora, huh?"

"Yes, sir. He wanted to be let off in a pizza restaurant instead of a house or apartment."

"Do you recall the name of this pizza restaurant?"

"It was Little Something. It had Little in the title. Little Julio's? I'm not sure, sir."

"That's OK. What did this man talk about? Was there anything odd about him?"

"He didn't talk very much. One odd thing. He liked to point out the different trees as we drove along."

Broadscale smiled. "Trees, huh. Well, thank you for your time, Mr. al-Ghazzawi, you have been very helpful."

"You are welcome, sir. Tell me, what did this man do? Am I in any danger?"

"He's wanted for questioning. I can't elaborate at the moment. The investigation is ongoing," Broadscale said. "But, no, I don't think you are in any danger. Here … take my card. If something pops up or if you remember the name of that pizza joint, please give me a call."

"Will do, sir. Oh, one other thing that I just thought of. After I dropped him off and was pulling away, I looked in my rearview mirror. It looked like this guy threw away a briefcase."

"That *is* interesting. Thanks for letting me know."

Broadscale walked back to his dark sedan and made a call. "Looks like we're going to Eudora, Mississippi."

## CHAPTER 47

By the time that Memphis FBI office had formed a team to travel to Eudora, the guns had returned. For most of the nation anyway.

Gun stores again had inventory. Gun manufacturers could again crank out death. Police and private citizens—which included gangs and militia groups as well as hunters and sportsmen—once again had access to their lost possessions.

News crews were quick to get their "man on the street" reactions. Those Americans who had closeted in their homes for safety were jubilant; some reportedly fired their weapons into the air, as if bullets were not subject to gravity. There were injuries and homes were damaged. "I can't wait to get strapped and walk into Starbucks," said one Georgia man. "That'll show them snowflakes."

The NRA had no immediate comment.

Meanwhile, stunned gun control advocates urged immediate legislative action to re-create the relative calm of the past month. "For about thirty days, America was like the rest of the world. Almost nobody died because of a gun," said the spokeswoman for Moms Against Guns. "We have seen what the future could be. Let's make it the present."

At the White House, the president and his Cabinet took a cautious stance. "Despite the statement we put out, I can't say I'm happy to see people get their guns back. And there's no guarantee that the guns won't disappear again," said the president. "If it happened once, it can happen again. And this Radley or Roy fella hasn't been apprehended yet."

The FBI director spoke up. "I can tell you, Mr. President, that our agents are closing in on a site in Mississippi believe to be the residence of this Roy McDonald. We'll soon see what that turns up."

"Thank you, Mr. Director. So, what has been the reaction to the end of the missing gun crisis?"

"It's pretty early yet, Mr. President," said the chief of staff. "But indications are that there's substantial relief in some sectors, but, understandably, an equal amount of concern in others. Some folks seem to have forgotten what happened—and didn't happen—over the past month or so. And some folks won't ever forget it."

"I see," said the president. "What about our foreign friends?"

The secretary of State said, "They are equivocating as per usual. They see the good and the bad of having four hundred million guns suddenly reappear. Several European diplomats have told me that they hope we've learned a lesson."

The Defense secretary added, "I can assure you that most of our allies are happy to see us making guns again. To quote one of my European colleagues, 'It is growing tiresome seeing all the crazy in America.'"

The Homeland Security director, knowing his turn would soon come, raised his hand. "Mr. President, if I may. We have already had reports of the first gun deaths since the, uh, crisis began. Several of these were gang related in LA and Chicago, and one incident was a domestic shooting in Iowa. We are also receiving reports about a number of gun-related suicides. However, on the plus side, it appears cross-border traffic has ebbed a bit. And given your concern, Mr. President, it might be too early for the states that deployed National Guard units to have them stand down. At least until we see where we are."

"Thanks for your summation," said the president, turning toward

## CHAPTER 47

the chief of staff. "You know, this might be the right time to reintroduce our gun-control legislation to Congress. Ban those assault weapons and cop-killer bullets. After what we've seen over the past month, I think we could get universal background checks passed."

"We'll get on it, Mr. President. Anything else?"

"Yes," the president said. "How about introducing a law that would require members of Congress have to serve as pallbearers the next time there's a school shooting."

Silence.

"All right. Wishful thinking and all that. Everyone be vigilant, and I'll want an update tomorrow," said the president.

## CHAPTER 48

As America returned to its old normalcy of blood, fear, and death, the investigation into the mysterious Radley Duvall continued to be muddled. The dots just wouldn't connect.

Agent David Broadscale had made the FBI's Memphis office his base while trying to piece together the Washington-Memphis-Eudora linkage. A check of motorcycle owners in DeSoto County had not been fruitful so far. The pizza restaurant mentioned by the driver, Raisul al-Ghazzawi, turned out to be Little Mario's, an easy find as it was the only pizza joint with "Little" in its name in DeSoto County. However, the restaurant had closed by the time Raisul made his dropoff. There were no witnesses, no one to question. Another dead end.

The Memphis staff had given Broadscale a small, unused office. At least it had a desk, a phone and a computer, he reconciled. He was sitting at his desk and looking over his notes. *What have I missed*, he thought, tapping his pen in a steady beat on the morning newspaper someone had tossed on his desk. It was the latest edition of the Commercial Appeal. Broadscale rubbed his eyes with his left hand, then looked down at the newspaper. He glanced at the large front-page photo and story underneath it. It was what his journalist

## CHAPTER 48

friends would call a "main module." Broadscale sat upright, dropped his pen and grabbed the paper with both hands.

The photo was of little Krissy Middleton playing in her backyard in Dubuque, Iowa. The story was what the journalists call a "follow-up." The paper had sent one of its reporters from Memphis to Iowa to see how Krissy was faring in the aftermath of her "miracle" cure. By all accounts, she was doing well; the effervescent child had already returned to her school. Doctors could find no residual signs of her cancer. Krissy told the reporter that her parents were planning a big party for her birthday. "I hope I get a dog for my birthday," she told the reporter. "I've never been able to have pets before."

After consuming the article, Broadscale wrote MEMPHIS on his notepad and circled it. *The "Memphis Miracle." Duvall flew to D.C. from Memphis, and then another miracle, if you can call it that, occurred there,* Broadscale thought. *Maybe Memphis is at the center of this. Maybe these miracles are the key.*

Broadscale went to his computer and downloaded a dozen or so articles about the overnight cures at St. Jude's. He jotted down the names of the six children who had, as one St. Jude's official put it, "been touched by God," as well as the name of the doctor seen leaving the unit that night on hospital cameras—Dr. Miguel Rosario. Broadscale then called a half dozen agents—some from Memphis, some from Washington—into his office.

"I need you to interview these six children. These are the kids who were cured at St. Jude's. The hospital should have contact info for them," Broadscale said, handing out sticky sheets to the six agents. "We need to find out if they saw anyone that night. Did anyone enter their rooms. If so, can they describe them. Questions?"

"No sir," was the collective response. The six agents began dispersing toward their cubicles to hit the phones.

"Get back to me as soon as you find anything. I'm going to talk to this Dr. Rosario myself."

Broadscale called St. Jude's and was pleased to learn that Dr. Rosario was on duty that morning. About an hour later, the two men were sitting across from one another in the doctor's office, both struggling to nurse the machine coffee Rosario had bought.

Broadscale placed his phone on the doctor's desk. "You don't mind if I record this conversation, do you?"

"Not at all," replied the doctor. "I'm not sure how much help I can be. I was not actually here when everything ... happened."

"As I understand it, the hospital security cameras have you entering in the wee hours that night and then leaving about an hour later." The agent pulled out a still photo of "Rosario" from the security footage and placed it before the doctor.

The doctor sat forward. "As I told the Memphis police, that is not me in that video. I was home asleep with my wife. I know it looks like me, but it's not me, I assure you. If I could cure kids of cancer by just walking by, I would be doing so today."

"I'm sure you would," said Broadscale. "So, do you think this is an impersonator?"

"It must be."

"Any idea who it might be?"

"I have thought about that, trust me. No, I have no clue," the doctor said. "In some ways this person was very good in impersonating me, but in other ways there were a bit sloppy."

"What do you mean?" asked the agent, suddenly intrigued.

"Your photo is a very good reproduction. I salute the FBI's technology. So, look here," Rosario said, pointing to the head of the man in the picture. "The face is mine but look at the hair. It is much darker than mine is now."

Broadscale made a quick comparison. "I'd say you're right."

"Now, look at this," said the doctor, who then pulled a St. Jude's promotional brochure out of his desk. He flipped a few pages and stopped on a page bearing head shots of the hospital staff. "See anything interesting?"

The agent looked at the brochure and then back at his photo. He looked again to verify what he saw. "You're right. The hair is the same in that brochure picture."

"This brochure is over five years old," said Rosario. "I'm a bit older and grayer now, as you can see. This same photo is still up on our website. I think whoever the impersonator is, they used this old photo in order to make their disguise."

## CHAPTER 48

"That's very interesting, doctor. Can I have that brochure?"

"Certainly."

The agent and the doctor chatted for a few more minutes; Broadscale learned from him the identity of the nurse who had been at the admissions desk that night. He took closeups of the two pictures, then called the nurse, awakening her from her slumber. He then texted her the two photos. She agreed that the man she saw was more like the younger Rosario. "But it was only a quick glance," she said. "I don't know if I'd make a good witness."

"That's OK," Broadscale said. "I appreciate your assistance."

Once back in his office, Broadscale consulted with his team of agents. "Anybody get anything we can use?"

Five of the agents said the children they spoke with—even newspaper cover girl Krissy—slept through the night and didn't notice anything until the next morning. Only one of the agents reported a different account. "This kid from Buffalo, Devontae Washington, said he heard a sound and then saw what he called the 'outline' of someone in his room. But he was half asleep and didn't get a good look. He said doctors and nurses were always coming into his room in the middle of the night, so he didn't think anything of it."

Broadscale nodded at the agents. "Thanks, guys. Type up your notes and email them to me. Good work."

He sat down, leaned back and put his hands behind his head. *Miracles in two places. Impersonators. This case is getting curiouser and curiouser*, Broadscale thought.

## CHAPTER 49

Local and state police, along with volunteer search parties, scoured the area where Roy disappeared for days, but no trace of him could be found. His cellphone could not be located. There was no evidence of foul play, but no hints at Roy's whereabouts as well. The nearest possible witnesses, the workers at Little Mario's, had not seen anything out of the ordinary.

While the local authorities and Ellie's friends concentrated on the wooded area near where the scooter was found, the FBI concentrated on the RV park. The Memphis FBI team found that the odd-looking RV used by Roy McDonald had been the victim of a small explosion, causing it to burn down to the wheel hubs. It offered no other useful clues. Through questioning some of the longtime residents, the agents did learn that the RV previously housed two other people at one time, but that pair had left months ago. There didn't appear to be anything suspicious about them, said Jonnie Barnes Sr., the park manager. "Just a shy guy and a pregnant lady," he told them.

As for Roy, his neighbors described him as friendly and helpful, although a bit on the bookish side. "Always hauling up plants and such on that scooter of his," one said. "Smart fella though. Used a lot of those twenty-five-cent words." Another said, "He used to hang

## CHAPTER 49

out a lot with Ezra Hopkins at the old Waffle Barn. Anybody who was a friend of Gator's would be a friend of mine."

The FBI investigation had already uncovered a long paper trail, but the D.C. agents could not find anyone in Washington or elsewhere who actually had a one-on-one relationship with Roy outside of Mississippi. There were no relatives, no school chums. Questions only led to more questions. It was as if Roy McDonald never existed.

Special Agent Thomas Dettwiler with the Jackson field office stopped by Ellie's home to ask some questions and perhaps offer some resolution.

"Don't be nervous, Miss Atkinson. This is just some follow-up we're doing. You seem to be the only person on the planet who knows Mr. McDonald," said Dettwiler.

"Well, we have been dating for a few months. Roy is one of the kindest, sweetest men I have ever met. He treated me like a princess," Ellie said.

"That's good to hear. But I may have some bad news. It appears you might be the victim of a scam," the agent said.

"A scam?"

"That's right. Or something akin to one. You said this Roy McDonald was a botanist contracted with the Department of Agriculture."

"That's what he told me. He had an ID and papers, and he showed me some of the plant samples he was running tests on."

"The Agriculture Department has no record of any such a contract in Eudora or anywhere in the state. Not with a Roy McDonald or anyone else. In fact, there are no ongoing federal contracts at this time in the Eudora area."

A stunned Ellie sat silent.

"Did he try to get anything of value from you?" the agent asked.

"No. Never. He paid for almost everything." The real Ellie then returned for a moment. "How much does a third-grade teacher have anyway."

"Good point. You mentioned some plant experiments. Were any of those plants ..."

"Marijuana?"

"Right."

"No. And, yes, I know what pot looks like. Don't ask me how," she said. "He told me they were aquatic plants."

"That RV he was living in ... did he ever talk about the antenna array that was attached to it."

"Roy just said it was for measuring climate change. He recently went to Washington to do a presentation on climate change in Mississippi. Why?"

"Climate change, huh. Well, we can't figure out much from what was left. It was all a molten mess. Kind of unusual for a botanist, don't you think?"

"I wouldn't know."

Dettwiler asked her about Roy's connection to Ezra and about the nature of their relationship. She was as honest as possible, but naturally she held back a few personal details. She described their trip to Memphis and revealed what she knew about Roy's last trip to Washington.

Dettwiler stood. "I think that's all the questions I have at this time. Here's my card if you can think of anything or if he contacts you."

"Contacts me? What do you mean?"

"This is still listed as a missing persons case, Miss Atkinson. We have no evidence of anything more than that at present. I can tell you that Mr. McDonald is a person of interest in a related investigation we are conducting."

"There's a second investigation?" asked Ellie, standing to see the agent out. Gator came bounding over and put his paws on her pant leg.

"Yes, ma'am. That's all I can say. That's a cute little fella," said Dettwiler, scratching Gator's head before opening the door.

"Yes, he is. Roy found him. Saved his life," Ellie said, picking up Gator and cradling him in her arms. "How could anyone who could save a little dog be guilty of anything?"

"I don't know, Miss Atkinson. I only follow the evidence. Have a good day, now."

## CHAPTER 49

Ellie stood just inside the doorway as the agent departed. She felt one part embarrassed, one part angry and one part … what? The latter she would have to come to terms with.

## CHAPTER 50

The Mississippi authorities soon gave up the search for Roy, needing to turn their attention to a wave of new shootings in the wake of the return of the guns. There were more mass shootings now than before "the disappearance."

Ellie's school supervisors gave her some time off as "mental health days." She continued to come to the scooter site for several more days. It was almost March, but the chill still had a bite. *First Ezra, now Roy.* Ellie looked skyward. *Please tell me. Who up there did I piss off?*

At home, Ellie continually failed to find distraction. The only time she felt human was when she looked into Gator's deep brown eyes. It was if the dog was asking her how he could bear the hurt for her.

"You miss him, too, don't you?" she said. Gator's tail wagged slowly. "He was the one who found you, you know. He brought you home and gave you a name."

Ellie sighed. She didn't feel like eating dinner, particularly not alone after all the months Roy was around. But she needed to find another way to keep on living, keep on moving forward. She put Gator on a leash, went outside and opened the garage door to enter

## CHAPTER 50

her "studio." She wrapped Gator's leash around a bench post and put down an old towel as a bed. Since the paint fumes from some of the oil prevented her from shutting the garage door, she turned on a couple of electric space heaters to keep it tolerable.

She then flipped on the radio, already set to an oldies rock station, hoping some familiar voices would help. Mick Jagger began to belt out the opening refrain to "Sympathy for the Devil." *Figures*, Ellie thought.

She set a fresh canvas on the easel and prepared the surface to accommodate her brush. Then she squeezed a variety of oil colors onto her palette, mixing some brown with a bit of black and a touch of yellow. She turned to the canvas and began creating some land areas to contain the wild Mississippi stream she was about to create. Ellie took a new brush and mixed some blue and white to form the water.

Out of the corner of her eye, she noticed Gator straining against his leash. The little dog began to bark, so she turned to see a figure holding a flat box.

"Why hello there, Miss Atkinson," Roy said. "Pizza's here."

## CHAPTER 51

A few days before, the Xylodonian recovery craft made a scheduled stop at Neptune Station—Base Buc-ee's, some of the older Guardians were calling it. The flight had been a quiet one; the two novice Guardians had bound Anton and kept him sedated in a holding room for the entire trip. They could monitor him via cameras, but there was no need. He barely moved.

They landed in one of the station bays, powered down the craft and set about preparing the prisoner. Their orders were to turn Anton over to Protectorate authorities on Neptune, then they were to assume his surveillance mission on Earth within the same region.

Hand weapons drawn, the Guardians entered the holding room and released Anton from his bonds. Only now, far beyond Earth range, it wasn't Anton they confronted.

"Where the fuck am I? Who are you assholes?" said a dopey and dazed Jonnie Barnes. The two Guardians looked at one another, imagining the Xylodonian equivalent of guillotine blades hanging above their heads.

"It's a human," said one of the Guardians.

"Damn right I am. What the hell else would I be?" snarled Jonnie.

## CHAPTER 51

"Wait. You two ain't human. Oh, fuck. Is this an alien abduction? I don't want you assholes experimenting on my…."

A Guardian sedated Jonnie.

Yordan-44, the executive officer of Neptune Station, was summoned to the ship. "What seems to be the problem?" he asked the Guardians.

"Sir, somehow an error has occurred. We were ordered to collect and retain Centurion Guardian Anton-7. We went to the coordinates provided and were given the proper signal. We then beamed Anton-7 aboard our vessel. Following Protectorate orders, we sedated and bound the returnee. He was placed in a holding room and fed via injection. We had no direct contact with the returnee until landing at Neptune Station. When we came to get him, we found this."

Yordan looked at the slumbering human. "You say he resembled Anton-7 when you brought him on board?"

"Yes, sir."

"Well, this is clearly not Anton. It appears some type of subterfuge is at play here. I think I know what happened, and if I'm right, this could be serious."

"What do we do with the returnee … uh, prisoner … sir?"

"Let's place him … it is a *him*, right? You never know with humans … in a station holding cell for now until we get further instructions. Obviously, you can't take him back."

The slumbering Jonnie Barnes was dragged away. There would be no more pre-dawn window-peeping for him, at least for the time being; the only peeping would be from the other side of his cell door.

Yordan and the two chagrined Guardians then activated a communications link with Sub-Protector Korphan.

"*Girgach,*" he screamed.

"We are sorry, sir," said the senior of the two Guardians. "We had hoped that our first mission for Xylodon would be a success. We are ashamed to have let you and our planet down."

Korphan paused to still his temper. "Fine, then. An experienced officer took advantage of you. You two *nimnules* should have never agreed to his alternative pickup plan. I won't recommend any form of punishment over this lapse, but it will go on your service records."

"Understood, sir," said the Guardian. "Is there anything we can do to remedy this?"

"No, first we must find Anton. I don't care that the situation on Earth appears to have changed. He'll have to answer for it," said the sub-protector. "I suppose there's nothing to do now but wait. We'll have to see if he tickles the web of one of our operatives.

Yordan asked, "And what do we do with the human, sir? He's seen far more than … is practical."

"Yes, that is a problem," said Korphan. "Hold him for now and let me send the matter up the chain to get some sort of consensus on what to do."

"As you wish, Sub-Protector," said Yordan. "And when we find Anton?"

"Then, we'll act. Once and for all time."

## CHAPTER 52

Roy caught Ellie before she hit the garage floor, but the palette and easel went flying. Gator jumped up and down in excitement.

He placed her on her swivel stool—then caught her hand before she could slap him.

"Where … have … you … been?" she demanded between sobs.

Ellie rose and hugged Roy tightly. She took his face in both hands and kissed every part of it.

"I'm so glad you're back and OK." She looked up at him. "Promise you will never leave me. Promise."

"I promise," he said, using a finger to wipe away tears.

Ellie regained some bits of her composure, but her expression demanded an explanation.

Roy paused, then bent over to pat Gator.

What he had come up with to tell her was that Jonnie Barnes and three other men had kidnapped him and held him in a hunting shack in the woods until a couple days ago. The four men had run him off the road and grabbed him because they thought he had access to government drugs. He was then going to explain that he managed to get away when the four found some real drugs and passed out. Finally, he was going to say he spent the last few days wandering in the Mississippi wilderness until he found Highway 304.

What he wasn't going to say was that portraying Jonnie Barnes for nearly two weeks was a colossal pain in the ass. But on the way to Ellie's house, he had reservations about that explanation; she would have too many questions. He imagined the conversation going like this:

"But you work for the Department of Agriculture," she said. "Why would they think you had drugs?"

"As Ezra might say, they weren't the brightest bulbs on the tree. Apparently, Jonnie had stolen a package from the RV with some lab glassware in it. He and the other geniuses thought chemical beakers equated to a drug lab."

"What happened to your RV? We found it burned to the ground."

"I can't say for sure. One of Jonnie's guys said they had covered up their tracks. I guess that means they burned it."

"Have you gone to the police? Do we need to go now?"

"I prefer that we leave the police out of it."

"Why? You were kidnapped. They were probably going to kill you and leave you in the woods. They could do this to someone else. We have to contact the police."

Anton knew that this is where his "Roy/Jonnie" story would fall apart. It raised too many suspicions.

The time had come to roll the dice.

"You need to sit down," he said, placing Ellie on her stool. "There's more to the story. And no matter what you hear, please know that I love you. That's probably been the case since the first moment I saw you in Waffle Barn. I have never met anyone as beautiful inside and out."

"I feel the same way, as if you couldn't tell. So, I guess you better start from the beginning."

"Do you want to go inside. Might be more comfortable."

"No, right here's fine. I like having a big open door in case I need to run."

# CHAPTER 52

"Well, you might want to after you see what I show you. OK," he said, touching his watch. "First of all, my real name is not Roy …"

Anton switched to his Xylodonian humanoid shape, smaller than the average human and completely hairless. Not unpleasant, but different. His human clothes were baggy on his frame. "Hi. I'm Anton. Pleased to meet you."

"Oh, my freaking God. What the hell are you?"

Anton gulped. He quickly switched back to his "Roy" shape. "Please don't be frightened. I think you—meaning all mankind—have long been aware of the possibility of other life forms in the universe. I guess I'm proof that that supposition is correct."

"Where are you from and why are you here?"

Anton launched into a description of Xylodon and its similarities and differences from Earth. He described its features and its people. He tried to explain some of its technological advances, but Ellie wrinkled her brow. He told her that war and most violence is non-existent there and that education and scientific achievement are held in esteem—making sure to emphasize the education part. Anton repeatedly tried to assure her that his mission was a peaceful one. Oddly, Ellie didn't seem overly surprised by his explanation.

"Xylodon is much drier than Earth. That's the reason that I and others like me are here, to study how Earth creates and conserves water. I actually am very interested in climate change."

He didn't mention the surveillance part of his mission.

"Others like you?" said a suddenly alarmed Ellie. "How many others like you are here?"

"I honestly don't know. There are research teams scattered about the planet. We act independently of each other with little communication between us. Most of our communication is with supply vessels that dash in and out. Those are likely your infamous UFO sightings. I had two companions with me, as you know, but they left. And left me."

"They were Xylodons, too?"

"Xylodonians. Yes."

"What do you mean they left you?"

"I was supposed to return with them. But Termas and Zephyra—

my companions—were a couple. Zephyra was impregnated while here on Earth and was experiencing a complication gestation, as I understand it. Termas is a nervous sort. I'm guessing he departed for our home planet because of her. I can't say for sure because I have not had contact with them."

"Are you really a botanist?"

"Yes, although I have a variety of duties, my primary classification is that of botanist. The plant life on Earth is wonderful and so varied compared to …"

Ellie cut him off. "Let me get this straight. You and your friends came here to look at plants. But your woman friend got herself pregnant, and her husband or companion or significant other or whatever went freaky and just left you here? That's pretty thin, mister."

"When you say it like that, I would have to agree," said Roy, trying to avoid Ellie's judgmental gaze. There was silence for a moment, except for Gator's whimpering. Ellie unleashed him and put him in her lap.

Finally, Ellie broke the quiet. "OK, so where have you been and what happened in the time since I saw you last?"

Roy's throat suddenly felt dry. "May I have some water?"

"There's a water bottle on the bench. It's yours now."

"Thank you, Ellie," said Roy, gathering his thoughts. He took a long swig from the plastic bottle.

"Well?"

"OK. What I am about to tell you may be a bit hard to believe."

"Oh, wow. Like a shape-shifting alien standing in my garage is easy to believe."

"Touché. I received a communication from my superiors that a vessel was being sent to pick me up. But, Ellie, I didn't want to go," he said, looking into her eyes.

"Why didn't you want to go home?"

"Home," he said, shaking his head. "Xylodon doesn't feel like home anymore. My home is where you are."

Ellie looked away and said nothing. She rubbed Gator's head.

"That's the main reason I want to stay. You have to believe me," he said. "But there is something else."

# CHAPTER 52

"Something else? What else, E.T.?"

Roy smiled thinly at the reference. *Wow, she's quick—and tough*, he thought. But he appreciated that Ellie was allowing him to explain. "I was in a bit of trouble. Still am probably."

"With who? What did you do? Shoot death rays at the White House?"

Roy frowned at Ellie's attempt at humor. "Not exactly. My supervisors probably think it's worse than that. What I did I felt I needed to do, but it could have jeopardized the entire mission and my colleagues. It still might."

Ellie gave an impatient circular gesture with her hand, signaling him to continue.

"I took away America's guns."

Ellie's jaw dropped. "YOU WHAT? *You* are the one who did that? You? By yourself? You made the guns disappear? Why?"

"It was because of Ezra," he said, his voice slightly cracking. "And you. And your kids. I got tired of the bodies and the blood."

He then explained how he entered the Capitol and managed to get into the House hearing room. Using his watch, he gave Ellie a demonstration of how Radley Duvall came into being and—with another twist of the watch—how he made his escape as a young Black boy. Roy then went into the weeds of how the RV's antenna array, coupled with his watch and rings, were able to create the mass illusion of guns disappearing and how he was able to exclude the U.S. military from the effects.

"So, for a bit more than a month, nobody died in America from a gun," he said.

Ellie sat disbelieving. "You have the power to do that?"

"Yes. Well, me and my little friend here," he said, nodding at his watch.

"Why, oh, why did you bring them back? The guns, I mean."

"I didn't have much choice. I had to destroy the RV and its antennas before the rendezvous. Losing the antennas reduced the illusion effect to a much smaller radius. Trust me, I hated to do it. I can only hope that Representative Babaloux was in an airport TSA line when her .32 pistol reappeared."

"Now, that would be karma," said Ellie, making a prayer gesture while balancing Gator. "And that's right. You said one of your Xylophone ships was coming to pick you up."

"Xylodon."

"Whatever. What else haven't you told me?"

Roy tapped his watch once again. "Meet Jonnie Barnes."

He outlined how he pulled off the switch and outwitted the Xylodonian Guardians. "I imagine they had quite a surprise at some point. But trust me, living as Jonnie Barnes for two weeks was no easy task. His father snores and farts as he walks, and they eat nothing but crap. I couldn't wait to leave."

"Yet another getaway. How did you pull that off?"

"Let's just say that Jonnie Barnes left his father a note saying he and some buddies were headed to Las Vegas," Roy replied. "What's the saying? What goes to Vegas stays in Vegas, or something like that."

"Holy shit. You really thought this whole thing through, didn't you?" Ellie said with a hint of admiration.

"I attempted to. Did you ever see the cartoon about Bugs Bunny and the Martian? (Ellie nodded her head affirmatively) Making the firearms go away likely made my superiors 'vewwy angry.' Not getting on the return craft likely made them 'vewwy vewwy angry'."

Ellie couldn't help but chuckle at Roy's Martian imitation. "He sounds more like Elmer Fudd than Marvin the Martian. Look, this is a lot to handle. I have to confess that I am having a hard time wrapping my head around all of this."

"Uhhh ... there's a bit more."

"MORE?"

"Remember those six kids at St. Jude's who were suddenly cured? That was me."

"You got rid of their cancer? How did you pull that off as well?"

"Yes, Miss Atkinson. I decided that having six healthy kids was a good trade for six people killed at Waffle Barn. I think Ezra would, too. You can take a lot of the credit. You were the one who planted the seed of an idea in my head when we drove by there. Well, that and the movie theater ad." Roy, pleased that he was able to squeeze

## CHAPTER 52

in a botanical reference. He then detailed how the all-night escapade at St. Jude's went down, including his impersonation of Dr. Rosario.

Ellie set Gator down and put her face in her hands, shaking her head back and forth. "Guns. Kids. Jonnie Barnes. UFOs. Anything else?"

"No, there's nothing else, Ellie. I want you to believe that. You are the reason I am here now. My life would be nothing but emptiness without you in it. It would like one of those black holes near …"

Ellie cut him off. She smiled.

"Roy, just shut the hell up." She looked into his eyes and gave him a kiss. Then she stepped back.

She tapped her watch.

## CHAPTER 53

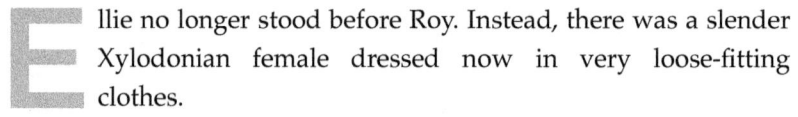

Ellie no longer stood before Roy. Instead, there was a slender Xylodonian female dressed now in very loose-fitting clothes.

Confused, Gator issued a low growl.

Even more confused, a jaw-dropped Roy took a few steps back.

"Hi. I'm Juleetha-6. Pleased to meet you." Juleetha again tapped her watch, which Roy had never really noticed, and she was Ellen Atkinson once again. That seemed to make Gator happy.

Roy/Anton gaped in a stunned silence.

"For once you have nothing to say," she chortled. "Now I know how to shut you up. And now you know why I didn't just jump up and run away when you changed forms and started talking about spaceships."

"I had no clue whatsoever. Wow, what a *nimnule* I am," said Roy. "Did you know that I wasn't human?"

"I knew it almost immediately."

"How? What gave it away?"

She pointed at his watch.

"You never noticed that I recognized it. I have found the male of our species to be just as narrowly focused as human males,

## CHAPTER 53

especially after they have had a whiff of … well, you know," she said.

He had no suitable answer for that. "Guilty. But now it's your turn to explain. And why did you let me go on and on about Xylodon for so long?"

"I was sent to Earth about four years ago. I was part of a team as well. We operated near the humans' NORAD facility in Colorado. The Protectorate was very curious about what went on there. As for your question, you were just so cute in your explanation. You should have seen yourself."

Now it was Roy's turn to pick up Gator. "So how did you get here?"

"My cover was that of a teacher. Makes sense, right? I grew to enjoy immersing myself with human offspring. They are like those unpainted canvasses over there," she said, nodding toward a garage corner. "They are so easily influenced by a kind word or encouraging gesture. They say anything and they feel everything. Anyway, when it came time to return to Xylodon, I didn't want to leave. So, I left Colorado and went into hiding."

Roy nodded his head. "I saw a report some time back about a Xylodonian deserter. We … uh, I … didn't believe it. Must have been a bureaucratic screw-up instead, or so we assumed."

Ellie frowned. "I don't like to think of it as desertion. I prefer to call it a life choice. I want to do something meaningful with my life. If I can teach children how to be kind and to be more accepting of others, then I will have accomplished much."

Roy well understood. He signaled for her to continue.

"I lived in a place called Hot Spring, Arkansas, for a time. The mineral springs there are wonderful. The people were generally friendly, but the town wasn't rural enough. Plus, I read in a history book in the Hot Springs library about nine Black children who were not allowed to go to school. The military had to be summoned so that these children could enter a place to learn. It was so unlike our planet! I promised myself that I would fight such hatred wherever I found it. So, I looked for a place where such hatred might still exist and was also out of the way. Mississippi was that place."

"There are a lot of places in Mississippi you could go to. Why Hernando?"

Ellie smiled. "Ezra. I was driving through and got a flat tire on the interstate. Guess who stopped and helped me change the tire?"

"Ezra. Naturally."

"So, I stuck around. Rented this house. Applied at the school district," she said with a mischievous expression. "The district seemed pretty happy to have a warm body interested in teaching here. With all the openings they had, they didn't look deeply into my credentials. And later on, I really did answer Ezra's ad. You pretty much know everything else."

"Wait a minute. I recall you saying that you were married for a short time, and that's how you ended up with the house." He gave her a faux suspicious glance.

"You caught me. That was a lie. I never gave you a name, so you couldn't look it up. It was just a way to explain how I got this place without raising questions."

Roy nodded. "Good cover. So, over all this time no one from the Protectorate has tried to contact you? Hunt you down?"

"Not so far. I got rid of all communications and tracking devices and created new paperwork for my background. I only kept this," she said, raising the wrist bearing her holo-watch. "But you, my friend, have authorities from two planets looking for you. The Protectorate is not going to be happy with the stunt you pulled, and an officer with one of the humans' elite police units, the FBI, has already been here once."

"Yes, I am well aware." Roy set Gator down and wrapped his arms around Ellie, melting into her. "You have no idea how much I have missed you. So, do I call you Ellie or Juleetha?"

"Ellie will do," burying her head in his shoulder. Roy savored the memory of the smell of her hair.

"Forgive me, but I have to ask," he said, partly not wanting the answer. "You have mentioned a few human men in your past. Is that where you got your, uh, education."

"No silly." Ellie chuckled. "That was just part of my cover. Earth

## CHAPTER 53

men are crude monstrosities. Except Ezra. Besides, I had some sort of hunch about you by our second meeting."

"Just call you Sherlock."

"And I have another little surprise for you." She moved to the rear of the garage toward a large cabinet bearing her various paint supplies and paint-smeared hanging clothes. Ellie turned a hook on the right, and the rear panel of the cabinet slid open. "Want to take a look at my sanctum sanctorum?"

Gator ran in before Roy could peer inside the darkened space. The thin chain hung from a bare bulb; Roy pulled the chain, illuminating a small space that held a fold-up cot, a small refrigerator, a fan, and a space heater. There was a damp, musty smell. Roy turned to Ellie with a curious look.

"I call it my 'just in case' room. Just in case someone shows up who I don't want to talk to. I've only been back here once since we got Gator. He didn't like it, inside or out."

Roy turned off the light and stepped and gave Gator a look. The dog cocked his head as if saying, "Who? Me?"

"That could be pretty useful. Good to know it's there. So now what?" he asked.

Ellie took his face in her hands. "Now what? First, go order us a fresh pizza, and then we'll figure out 'now what'."

## CHAPTER 54

"Folks, it's imperative that we the United States obtain this technology," said the president told his national security team gathered in the Oval Office. "And we need to get it before our adversaries do."

His chief of staff passed some documents across the Resolute desk. "Sir, there are many indications now that the guns did not disappear but were only hidden in some way."

"Gone. Hidden. Doesn't really matter, does it? Look at the magnitude and duration of this event. Imagine the advantage we'd have if we can make another country think it was unarmed for a month," the president said. "There's a good chance they'd surrender. There'd almost be no need for actual combat."

The National Security director concurred. "Yes, sir. And if we could determine how our military was excluded from the effects of this anomaly then perhaps it could be reverse engineered. Apply it only to the military of an adversarial nation or to regions exhibiting largescale terrorist activity."

"Yes, yes. That would be quite a boon wouldn't it," said the president. "Of course, our friends across the aisle would probably like to see us use it on Chicago and Detroit first."

# CHAPTER 54

The FBI director took his pipe from between his teeth. "It doesn't help that we have seen gun violence in many major cities return to levels approximating those before the crisis. Fortunately, we have dodged any mass shootings so far."

"We can probably dispense with the crisis label now," said the president. "Now that you've spoken up, continue. What is the status of our search for Duvall or McDonald or whoever he is?"

The FBI chief took a sip of the robust White House coffee and addressed the room. "Our agents have been working almost around-the-clock. The suspect, for lack of a better word at the moment, was traced to Memphis and then to a small community in central Mississippi. But there the trail runs cold. The man's motorbike was found abandoned alongside a road almost in the middle of nowhere. No blood, no sign of foul play. Interestingly, the RV vehicle the man was living in was turned into a virtual ash heap. It had to be high heat because much of the metal was molten. We weren't able to get much from that either. The folks in the RV park who had talked with him said he was smart, friendly, quiet. Essentially not the type who could wave a wand and make guns disappear."

"Where does that leave us?" asked the president.

"Sir, the suspect had a girlfriend, but she is the one who reported McDonald missing. She seemed quite distraught at his disappearance," said the FBI chief. "One of our Jackson agents has already paid her a visit and said he noticed nothing unusual."

The head of the National Security Agency added, "Sir, we have been monitoring signals traffic from that area for the past few days and have not found anything suspicious. Of course, that may be because we are late to the game."

"Thank you," said the president, turning again to the FBI director. "Any chance this girlfriend is in on it?"

"It appears unlikely from the first interview, sir, but she may be worth talking to again," he replied. "She looks like our only lead for now."

The president nodded. "If this McDonald has been grabbed by the Russians or Chinese, there could be hell to pay. I cannot stress strongly enough how important it is we keep him out of enemy hands. In whatever fashion that need be done."

His statement was met with a collective "yes, sir."

---

Millions of miles away, and unbeknownst to America, its concern had become a galactic concern as well—but for vastly different reasons. If human authorities were able to capture Anton, the entire Xylodonian operation on Earth could be in jeopardy. The network had taken decades to establish and had proven to be quite useful, not only for monitoring Earth's spaceflight programs but also for the knowledge obtained. Surprisingly, in some areas Earth science was almost equal to that on Xylodon.

Sub-Protector Korphan had presented the dilemma to the entire Protectorate Presidium, including mention of the human now being held on Neptune. There was a small faction that wanted to eliminate both Anton and Jonnie Barnes. Turning both to ash would solve all problems, they argued. There was another group that partly agreed, differing only by offering the humanitarian suggestion that Jonnie be sent to the Xylodon prison moon instead.

Now addressing the entire fifty-member Presidium in its massive chamber, Korphan said he was not opposed to the latter, but he cautioned the members that attempts to deal with the former—Anton—might attract unwanted attention on Earth. Even a win—removing or killing Anton—could put Xylodon at a disadvantage, he said.

The Praetor, the elected head of the Presidium, agreed. "That appears to be wise counsel, sub-protector. But if we are not going to eliminate this wayward Guardian in some way, then what do you recommend?"

"I do have an idea, Praetor, that could address all concerns. And the risk of exposure would be much smaller."

"Well then, Korphan, let's hear it."

"If the humans want Anton, let's give them Anton."

## CHAPTER 55

It was late March when the order came down. Spring was beginning to play maestro to a new sonata of rebirth and renewal across Mississippi and elsewhere.

Special Agent Thomas Dettwiler had barely poured his first cup of weak coffee and turned on his computer that morning. At the top of his email inbox was an item with an "Urgent" designation on the subject line. The message was not unexpected—it was surprising only in that it had taken this long to be sent.

Almost a week before this email arrived, Dettwiler had been contacted by Agent David Broadscale, who had just been recalled to Washington. Broadscale was uncertain there was a connection, but he felt the Mississippi ties to his case and Dettwiler's made it worth reaching out. Broadscale then emailed the Jackson agent with what his team had uncovered. It wasn't all that much, but it appeared highly coincidental.

"The most interesting bit is the claim by the St. Jude's doctor that he was impersonated by a younger version of himself," Broadscale told Dettwiler. "We weren't able to get the goods to back that up, but it might be one explanation for that Duvall character got out of the Capitol without being caught on camera."

Dettwiler thanked Broadscale, then collated the information from the two offices together, wrote a summary of their respective findings and submitted the package to his D.C. supervisors.

The message that finally arrived from Washington instructed him to obtain a search warrant for the Hernando, Mississippi, residence of one Ellen Atkinson. *About time*, he thought. *Those lard asses have too long out of the field — if they were ever there. They have been pretty slow to catch on to the fact that she's the only known connection to Roy McDonald.*

Dettwiler set about preparing the necessary paperwork to obtain a warrant. As long as he emphasized the national security implications involved, he shouldn't have much difficulty getting the warrant. He signaled for a young agent to take the documents to the Thad Cochran Federal Courthouse located on the aptly named Court Street.

That will take an hour or two, he figured, enough time to get a search team together. Just a few plainclothes boys should do it; no need for the FBI to take a public relations hit by calling out a SWAT team on a third-grade teacher. They had a van that would easily accommodate the five agents he had in mind.

He then had to make a courtesy call to the Hernando police department to let them know the FBI would be stepping on their turf. If everything went smoothly, they'd be in and out of Hernando before that night's NCAA basketball games.

Dettwiler took off his coat and loosened his tie. *Today's going to be a good day*, he thought.

---

It was late morning when Bobby Gene Holloway took the first bite of his cinnamon roll at the Country Skillet in Hernando. He liked the dark brew at the Skillet; it had a touch of Creole to it. Even though it had been weeks since he had resigned from the police force, Bobby Gene wasn't ready to start any serious job hunting. Images from the Waffle Barn continued to play out in a malevolent karaoke in his mind.

He instinctively looked up from the newspaper want ads when

## CHAPTER 55

he heard the entry door open. In came two Hernando police officers, both former colleagues and softball team members. They spotted Bobby Gene and signaled to the waitress that they would be joining him. They sat down and the waitress brought coffees over.

"How's it going, BG?" asked the large-bellied corporal. He'd been the catcher for the team. "Found anything yet?"

"Nothing yet. I would like to stay in this area," Holloway said. "Moving is a pain in the ass. Not a lot shaking around here though."

"I heard that," said the second patrolman. "And you don't earn much with just a high school diploma. That's why I'm in junior college."

The corporal blew on his coffee and took a sip. "You thinkin' about staying in law enforcement?"

"Part of me would like to," said Holloway. "But another part of me never wants to see again what I saw at the Waffle Barn."

Both uniformed officers nodded their heads. The officers then changed the subject to the department softball team, letting Boby Gene know that he was still welcome to play. They all had a second coffee and caught up on how things went when the guns were gone and general department gossip. There was a new dispatcher who was attracting quite a bit of attention. "She might be a lesbian, though," said the corporal. "She keeps putting off the single guys."

His radio squawked, and the corporal nodded his head to his partner that it was time to get back on the street. As they tossed down a few dollars for a tip, the corporal said, "Hey, didn't you go out with that teacher Ellie Atkinson for a while?"

"Yeah," said Holloway. "Nice gal. She got serious with another guy though. Why you ask?"

"The feds from Jackson are about to execute a warrant at her house. Some hullabaloo over her connection to that guy who made the guns go poof," said the corporal.

"That's odd. Two games of bowling was about as exciting as she got when we went out," Holloway said.

"Who knows?" said the corporal. "Probably just the feds trying to put on a show for Washington."

"Probably," Holloway said as the two officers headed to the door. "You boys be careful out there."

Bobby Gene sat back in his chair and watched the patrol car leave the parking lot. He then pulled out his phone.

## CHAPTER 56

Ellie, clad in a Southern Miss sweatshirt and some ripped gray sweatpants, was sitting on her porch when the van parked in her driveway. She had a glass of iced tea in her right hand and was holding Gator's leash in her left. Five men who looked like they stepped out of a khakis catalog got out the vehicle led by Special Agent Thomas Dettwiler. All were wearing sunglasses. Gator sensed that this was not a friendly visit and let loose his inner Chihuahua: Yap yap yap yap yap yap.

"Good afternoon, gentlemen. What can I do you for?" she said.

Dettwiler stepped around Gator and handed her some official looking documents. "Miss Atkinson, we have a federal warrant to search the premises. We would appreciate your cooperation."

"Weren't you just here a few weeks back? Didn't you have a look-around then?"

"Not really, ma'am. I only asked you a few questions. But now some new information has come to our attention," he said.

"What new information?"

"I am not at liberty to say. If you examine the warrant, you will see it gives us the right to look through your house, the garage and your car," Dettwiler said, assuming the alpha male role. "Are the garage and automobile unlocked?"

"The garage is unlocked; just lift the door. The car is locked. Let me get the keys," said Ellie, handing Gator's leash to Dettwiler. The four other agents chuckled into their hands.

She returned in a moment, handing the keys to Dettwiler, who then handed them to another agent. That agent opened all of the Tesla's doors, popped the trunk and began his search.

Dettwiler pointed at another agent and wagged his finger at the garage to set him in motion.

Ellie barked at that agent. "Be careful in there. That's my art studio. There's wet paint on some of the canvasses." The agent put his sunglasses on top of his head but didn't otherwise acknowledge her. He lifted the door and went in.

"All right, the rest of us can go through the house. We'll do our best not to damage anything," Dettwiler said.

"Why do I have my doubts. C'mon Gator, let's go watch the show," said Ellie, stepping inside and finding a chair in the den. She put the still not-too-happy Gator on her lap.

Dettwiler stood nearby as the remaining two agents went from room to room. The agent who went to the kitchen opened every cabinet door and every drawer. When he opened her flatware drawer, Ellie couldn't help herself, retorting, "I don't think anyone can fit in there."

The special agent shot her an annoyed glance. "Cute. We are not only looking for additional persons on the premises, Miss Atkinson. We are also looking for any evidence that you have had contact with Roy McDonald."

"I told you already I haven't heard from him. I thought you were still trying to find out how he disappeared."

"We are, and it's extremely important that we find him. He hasn't tried to call you?"

"No, and I'm pretty sure you knew that already," she said. "I'm guessing you have my phone records and have looked them over. You've probably peeped at my emails, too."

Dettwiler gave no response; instead, he removed the cushions

## CHAPTER 56

from the sofa. The other agents went methodically through Ellie's closets, bedroom and bathroom, pulling drawers, shoving clothes and looking in boxes and bins. Dettwiler looked under the throw rug in the den.

The agent who had searched the bathroom emerged with two toothbrushes. "Why the two toothbrushes?" he asked.

"As I explained to Agent Dettwiler, Roy was sometimes an overnight guest. I gave him his own toothbrush. As you can see, the bristles are dry."

"Why do you still have it out?" the agent volleyed, admiring his cleverness.

"Why has the mighty American government not been able to find Roy? Once you do, I will get rid of it." The agent reddened and went back to searching.

The agent who had searched the Tesla came inside the house. "Nothing unusual, sir. Unless you count Pink Floyd CDs."

"Hey, don't be dissing Pink Floyd," Ellie said in mock indignance. "It may be your head in a wall instead of a brick."

Dettwiler told the agent to go assist in the garage. He asked Ellie, "Is there an attic or basement?"

"No attic. No basement. The garage has some storage space up top where I put my holiday stuff. It's all open-air; you shouldn't need a ladder to see up there."

"Come with me," Dettwiler commanded, leading her outside and to the garage. He told the agents there to retrieve a few bins from the storage area and examine the contents. Just Christmas decorations and other holiday fare.

After more than an hour, the agents appeared satisfied. They didn't touch any of Ellie's wet paintings, but they didn't put back any of the drawers and sundry items they had pulled out. Her house was just shy of a mess.

"Thank you very much, Miss Atkinson," said Dettwiler, already trying to fashion his report to Washington in his mind. "Again, if you hear anything at all from Mr. McDonald or receive a clue as to his whereabouts, please give our office a call. You still have my card?"

"Yes, I do."

"OK, then. Let's saddle up, boys," he said. The agents put on their sunglasses and got into the van.

Ellie sat on the porch with Gator and waited for ten minutes after the G-men had left. Then she went into the garage, pulled down the door and walked to the storage cabinet. She tapped on the back wall, which slid open a moment later.

Roy gave her a kiss. "I guess your just-in-case room came in handy."

Ellie held a finger up to her lips as she stepped into the room. "Who knows if they planted bugs?" she whispered. "Let me give this place a good sweep (pointing at her watch) before we talk." She noticed that Roy had stretched out the cot. "Hmmmm. We could get kind of cozy in here."

"Why, Miss Atkinson, the things you do say," whispered Roy. "I guess it's a good thing you have old boyfriends."

Ellie punched his arm. "Bobby Gene's not a boyfriend, you jerk. Just a friend. Hey, at least I can make friends," she joked, not realizing at first that her offhand remark included Ezra. "Oops. Sorry. Please forgive me."

"It's OK. No harm, no foul."

The FBI agents had indeed examined Ellie's phone records and email accounts, finding nothing worth reporting. Had they looked at her recent online shopping activities, they might have found some unusual purchases from her Amazon account. Men's shirts and pants. Men's underwear and shoes. All those purchases were now piled in a corner of the secret room and all of which would have set off alarm bells if they had been noticed.

And, if the FBI agents had looked into Ellie's background with the same thoroughness they had applied to Roy McDonald they would have at least had more questions.

Ellie gave Roy a playful swat on the behind. "You know the routine. Be a good boy. Stay in here or the garage until dark, and then you can come out to play."

"Yes, Miss Atkinson. I can be your backdoor man."

She punched his other arm.

## CHAPTER 57

April arrived in its typical wet and wild fashion. The lingering chill and sporadic rains seemed to cool the hunt for Roy McDonald as well. The news media found themselves distracted by other events, such as the usual political shenanigans of the campaign primary season. Federal and state authorities had their hands full dealing with those who were celebrating the reappearance of their extended magazine, high-caliber crack pipes. A new baseball season had begun.

Business had been slow at Little Mario's on this midweek night, and A.J. Hartley was hoping to close early. He'd already let the other employees take off for the night. Having that kind of authority seemed kind of cool to the new twenty-two-year-old.

A.J. grabbed a mop and bucket from a closet and began combining soap and water, but he paused when he glimpsed a flash of light outside the restaurant. He thought it might be lightning or someone pulling into the parking lot with their high beams on, but when he looked out the window there was no vehicle to be seen. *That's odd*, he thought as he started mopping cheese, flour, and pepperoni off the kitchen floor.

A.J. was putting perishables into the refrigerator when the bell above the entry door announced someone had entered. He wiped his hands and came to the front counter, spotting a man about a decade or so older sitting at one of the tables. A.J. looked at the clock pushing 10 p.m.; the restaurant usually only received takeout orders after 9 p.m.

The customer looked like he had gone through the hardest of days, drawing a bit of empathy from A.J. He was pale and his clothes disheveled. Judging from his shoes, he had walked across Mississippi.

"Hi, there. We are just about to close up, so your choices are limited. I could probably put together a cheese or pepperoni pie for you," A.J. said.

The man sat silently, staring straight ahead with vacant eyes and rubbing his hands together. It seemed he was not only avoiding A.J., but he was shutting out the world as well. He was dead, yet not dead—like some of the zombies A.J. dispatched in his video games.

"Mister? Are you OK? I said our pizza choices are limited right now. Can I get you a glass of water or something?"

A.J.'s questions went unmet.

"Sir, if you are not going to order something, I'm going to have to ask you to leave," said an unnerved A.J.

The man mumbled something inaudible.

A.J. brought over a glass of water just to see what the man would do. It went untouched.

*OK, this is getting too creepy*, thought A.J. *Holy crap. What if this guy's had a breakdown? Or he's got PTSD from Iraq or Afghanistan or something?*

"Sir, just sit right there. I'll be right back." A.J. moved toward the back, but he kept the man within sight. He called 911, covering his mouth as he spoke. The dispatcher said a DeSoto County deputy would be there in a few minutes.

A.J. stood watching from this somewhat protected perch. The man had not moved, save for occasionally rubbing his wrist as if his watch was irritating the skin. "Sir, do you want a side salad or something else," he asked. No response.

A.J. then heard the familiar crunch of tires on gravel in the

## CHAPTER 57

parking lot, but he chose not to move forward. The door's bell dinged, and a deputy walked in. "Is this the man you called in about?" he asked A.J.

"Yes, sir. He came in about ten minutes ago and has been sitting there ever since. He won't talk and he hardly moves."

"Did he say anything or cause any disturbance when he came in?"

"No, sir. He just sat down and that's been it."

The deputy walked over to the man and snapped his fingers in front of his face. Again, no response. "Sir, are you OK? Feeling any pain?" Silence. The officer examined the man as best he could, not finding any obvious injuries.

"Sir, can you stand up." It was more of a command than a request. The deputy eased the man to his feet and began checking pockets for a wallet or possible identification. Finding none, he helped the man sit down again.

"Sir, what's your name?" asked the deputy. The question seemed to evoke a flicker in the stranger's eyes.

"Roy." The unexpected sound of the man's voice startled both the deputy and A.J. The deputy figured that if one cast worked, he might is well try another in the same part of the lake.

"Hello, Roy. Roy what?"

"McDonald. Roy McDonald."

"Roy, I am Deputy Hernandez with the DeSoto County Sheriff's Department. How are you feeling, Roy?"

The silence resumed.

The name had struck a chord of familiarity with the deputy, who then used his cellphone camera to snap a picture of the stranger. He texted the image into the Sheriff's Department and radioed his sergeant.

"Sarge, I think we have a mental health case over here at Little Mario's on 304. We've got a man who appears to be in some degree of distress. He doesn't have any ID, but he says his name is Roy McDonald. But that's all he'll say. Wasn't that the name of the guy who went missing about a month or so ago? I've texted you his picture. You might want to put it through facial recognition. Over."

Deputy Hernandez leaned against the counter and waited for a response. He continued to pepper Roy with questions to see if he could draw a reaction. The thousand-yard-stare routine continued.

When the sergeant responded, the urgency in his voice also raised the deputy's adrenaline. "Hernandez, we need you to hold that man right there. Don't let him out of your sight. We've got backup coming, and a team of feds will be meeting you back here."

"OK. Who is this guy? What has he done? Over."

"I can't say anything over open air. But it's a matter of national security. No matter what, keep that guy right there. Over."

A.J. had been eavesdropping. What he heard gave him an electric jolt. *Holy shit. National security. Did I just help catch a spy? I wonder if there is a reward.*

"Roger that," said Hernandez to his sergeant. He continued to stare at the stranger, who looked meek and defeated—anything but the Most Wanted Man in America. But that didn't stop him from unsnapping the strap on his holster.

## CHAPTER 58

It didn't take long for word about the apprehension of Roy McDonald to go up the federal food chain. As Special Agent Dettwiler and other agents sped toward DeSoto County—where a still silent Roy was now being held before an audience of two dozen local officers—the news went like a tongue of lightning through the forks of the federal government. First to the FBI director and the attorney, then to the CIA, NSA, and Pentagon. And then to the White House.

The chief of staff gently roused the president. "Sir, we've got him."

"Got who?"

"Roy McDonald, sir. The guns guy. He was found not far from where he went missing. Just walked into a pizza joint and basically turned himself in."

"Well, I'll be damned. Where is he now?"

"Local authorities have him in custody in DeSoto County, Mississippi. FBI agents from Jackson are on their way to secure him."

"Does the military need to be involved?"

"No sir, not at this time. But the folks from the National Security Agency are very eager to talk to him."

"That's the best news I've had in a while. Order us up some coffee. Call the usual suspects into the Situation Room. We've got some work to do."

---

The president was not the only one who was working late. At about that same time, a certain botanist and third-grade teacher were sitting on a den floor trying to determine their future.

Gator rolled over onto his back, paws wiggling in the air, inviting Roy to scratch his belly. Roy happily complied. Ellie sat cross-legged, flipping through a batch of travel magazines. The radio was playing softly on their favorite oldies rock station.

"As much as I would hate leaving Hernando and my kids, I think it's something we should consider," she said. "That FBI search was pretty nerve-wracking. We aren't likely to get a head's up if they come again."

"You mean from your Earth-cop boyfriend?" said Roy, not looking up. A magazine whizzed by his head.

"Pppfffffffttt. You know, I've been reading up on these Earth astrological signs. They appear to be mythological, but many humans believe these birth signs can shape one's personality. I think you must be a Scorpio. They never forget the tiniest slight throughout their lives."

"Hey, I can forgive. Eventually," he said.

"Uh-huh. What about that forget part? Scorpio is also the sign of romance and passion. In other words, horny bastards."

"I definitely represent that remark," he said, reaching over and sliding his hand up Ellie's bare leg.

"Calm down, you. Later. You need to pay attention."

"Oh, I'm paying attention all right." He leaned forward again—this time earning a swat from a magazine. He looked at Gator and made whimpering sounds.

As they chatted and plotted, "Take it Easy" by the Eagles began to play on the radio. The second stanza—a reference to the "fine

## CHAPTER 58

sight" that is Winslow, Arizona, or at least a corner of it—made Ellie sit up.

"That's it," shouted Ellie, so excited it made Gator jump. "Winslow, Arizona. Let's see here." She grabbed her laptop and commenced a search. "It's got a population of about nine thousand, and it has some top-rated schools. And look here (turning the laptop toward Roy), Arizona looks a lot like Xylodon. It's dry and rocky. That song was a sign, Roy."

"You could be right. It sure looks like I've found a lover who won't blow my cover. She's not hard to find at all."

"You, sir, have a one-track mind. The end of the school year is about a month away. I could turn in my notice, and we could head West, young man."

As they started to seal the deal with a kiss, the radio cackled.

*"We interrupt this program to bring you a special news bulletin. The man believed responsible for disappearance earlier this year of the nation's firearms has been apprehended in Mississippi. The FBI has identified the suspect as Roy McDonald of Eudora. That is all the information the FBI would release at this time. We repeat, the man believed responsible for the disappearance of the guns in America is now in federal custody. Continue to listen to this station for further updates. We return you now to our regular programming."*

Roy and Ellie looked at each another. "What the hell?" they said in unison.

---

The silvery-blue craft cruised behind Earth's moon. The far side of that moon allowed for undetectable communication.

"Neptune Station, come in. This is Guardian Rixfazz reporting. Come in, Neptune Station."

After a few moments, "This is Neptune Station. We read you, Guardian Rixfazz. What is your report?"

"Please inform the Protectorate that Operation Flip-Flop was a success. The humans have their human back. He was taken into custody, and it now appears Earth authorities have suspended further investigations."

"That's excellent news, Guardian Rixfazz. The Protectorate and the Presidium will be extremely pleased to hear this. So, there was no problem with his programming? He could only say the two words?"

"It appears there were no complications, Neptune Station. Yes, that was the extent of his vocabulary. By the way, the fake holo-biometrometer was a nice touch. The humans will have a vexing time with it."

"That's good to hear, Guardian. Sub-Protector Korphan gets the credit for that bit of subterfuge."

"One last question, sir. We often have contact with our other Earth operatives. What should we advise, should any of them make actual contact with Anton?"

"We have no instructions on that, Guardian. Please stand by." Neptune Station went silent for almost ten minutes before crackling back to life.

"Guardian, you are instructed to tell the Earth teams that for our purposes, Anton no longer exists. Is that clear?"

"Yes, Neptune Station, quite clear. Thank you. That's all we have for now. I will write a full report when we dock at Neptune Station. This is Rixfazz out."

"Safe journeys, Guardian. Neptune Station out."

# EPILOGUE

It took almost five months for Jonnie Barnes Sr. to become worried about his son. He figured Jonnie Jr. had plenty of wild oats to sow, so the lack of contact didn't worry him initially. But the boy had to have run out of money by now unless he'd hit a jackpot. That was unlikely; for one, Jonnie Jr. had the luck of a goat turd, and two, if he had hit something he would have called to rub it in his old man's face.

Barnes began to get an odd feeling in his gut. He filed a report with the Hernando police and gave them a photo of his son. It wasn't a great likeness, but family photos were never high on the priority list. The officer who took the report suspected Jonnie Jr. had become just another meth casualty, but he made a few inquiries to the various authorities in Las Vegas and Clark County, Nevada. After about a week, the Hernando officer got a call back. He scribbled a few notes, and then he called Jonnie Barnes Sr. and asked him to come in.

The old man entered the police station and was taken to an empty interview room. The officer handed Jonnie Sr. a Styrofoam cup of coffee, and they sat down at a beat-up Formica table. Jonnie

Sr. steeled himself for some bad news. What he hadn't prepared himself for was: no news.

"According to the folks out in Clark County—that's Vegas—no one by the name of Jonnie Barnes had checked into any of the main hotels. Now, that might not mean anything, because there are a number of under-the-radar establishments he might be staying at, if you get my drift."

"Uh-huh."

"Now, you say he drove out there with some friends? You have their names?"

"No, sir. The fellas he usually hangs around with are still in Eudora. He just left me a note and said he'd be back in a bit. Didn't say when or who he was traveling with."

"I also had the authorities out there check around the hospitals and emergency rooms. And the morgue. Nobody by the name of Jonnie Barnes was admitted to any of those, either. Again, it might not mean much. Something could have happened to them on the way out there. He ever go by any other names?"

"Nah, sir. Not that I know of anyway."

"Well, I gave them my contact information. If they get any leads, they said they will give me a call. I have also put out a nationwide BOLO—that stands for be on the lookout for—but I haven't had any hits yet. He does have a bit of a petty crime record, so he's not afraid of getting into mischief. If I hear anything, I will let you know. I have your number here. I have to be honest with you, after this amount of time, I wouldn't get my hopes up."

"Thank you, officer," Jonnie Sr. said, shaking the policeman's hand.

As he left the station, he shook his head. It was if Jonnie Jr. had fallen into the abyss that is the Vegas Strip. *He might as well have dropped off the face of the Earth,* Jonnie Sr. thought. He had no idea how right he was.

# EPILOGUE

The chief of staff to the president of the United States walked down a dark hallway in the bowels of an unnamed facility operated by the National Security Agency in Maryland. He was flanked by some dark-suited Ivy Leaguers armed with clipboards and cellphones. It was almost like a black site within a black site. The artificial lights seemed to be on their last ember, and the half dozen or so doors along the hallway carried no names or numbers. But the door they were looking for was easy to find; it had two guards with automatic weapons standing outside.

The chief nodded at the guards, one of whom opened the door for him. He entered a large room containing electronic and medical equipment. There was a small hallway to the left of the entryway that fronted a large glass window. The window provided a view into a smaller chamber within the larger sterile sanctum. The chief walked over to confer with some serious-faced men wearing white coats. The underlings—so determined by their lack of white coats—sat pecking away at computer terminals.

"Any change?" asked the chief.

"None at all," said White Coat No. 1. "Whenever he's asked a question, he keeps repeating the same two words: Roy McDonald."

"Has he responded to any of the ... uh ... medications?"

"No, sir. Not at all. We have tried changing the mixtures and the dosage, but so far, we've only gotten those two words out of him. He's non-verbal otherwise, but his vitals are good."

"Well, keep at it. We need to know who this man really is, and his fingerprints and DNA aren't in the system. He could be the key to some vital military secrets. Countless lives could depend on what's in this man's brain," said the chief. "Suffice to say the president is very interested."

"Yes, sir. We understand, sir," said White Coat No. 2.

The chief went down the hallway and peered into the smaller room. A pale hospital-gown clad man lay sleeping amid intravenous tubes and beeping machines. A third guard sat in a corner chair.

*Who are you, Roy?* thought the chief. *How did you make all the guns disappear?*

The Washington FBI "Illuminati" considered the case closed, but that didn't stop agents Dettwiler and Broadscale from emailing one another now and then. Dettwiler couldn't stop thinking about the Little Mario's angle. The man who was the most likely suspect in the Radley Duvall caper had been dropped off at Little Mario's. Then, someone named Roy McDonald first disappears near Little Mario's then reappears there unable to even howl at the moon. *There had to be something more to it than pepperoni*, he thought. Something else didn't quite add up as well—Ellie Atkinson had initially set a fire under DeSoto County authorities to search for Roy McDonald when he disappeared. But now that he was back, she had not once inquired about him. Didn't seem to care how he was doing or wonder where he was being kept. That seemed odd, but it wasn't a crime. *Not worth the gas from Jackson to Hernando to pursue it. At least not at the present time anyway*, he thought.

Broadscale kept having nagging thoughts about the photo of "young" Dr. Rosario. The man taken into custody looked nothing like the photo in his files. Of course, the man in the photos and the suspect didn't look a bit like Radley Duvall either. The FBI's digital imaging technology couldn't make a match to anyone at the Capitol that day the guns disappeared. The fake Rosario was in the wind, and there was no documentation on Roy McDonald or Radley Duvall. *What I have here are two ghosts and a zombie*, thought Broadscale. *Hard to make a case with that.* He took the photos and thumbtacked them to his bulletin board. *OK, guys. Gone for now, but not forgotten.*

---

Ellie Atkinson carefully arranged the erasers on the metal tray under the chalkboard. A new batch of third graders would come howling and scraping into the room when the next bell sounded. She and Anton had decided to stay in Hernando, at least for now. But that

# EPILOGUE

meant creating a new back story and paperwork for Anton. Roy disappeared.

Ellie checked the supplies in her desk but looked up—and smiled—when she heard some familiar sounds outside her classroom.

Principal Helene Appleberry clickety-clacked down the hall in Vince Camuto high heels and in full "Large Marge and in Charge" mode. She was the epitome of the alpha female.

It was the first day of the new school year at Hernando Elementary, and she didn't want any hitches. It was bad enough that the air-conditioning system was straining toward its demise. Then there was the shipment of first-grade primers that arrived late. And the two teachers who called in sick. At least one of them was probably nursing a hangover. It never ended.

Now, she had a neophyte second-grade teacher to break in. Yet another school district budget hire, but at least this one was husky, blond, and tanned. Smelled good, too.

"Here is the teacher's lounge, Michael. You can take your lunches in here or in the main lunchroom when you have cafeteria duty. Everybody pulls cafeteria duty. Trust me, you will find it a lot quieter in the lounge."

"Yes, ma'am."

Two boys came dashing down the hall and made a sliding stop at a restroom door. Books and backpacks added to the sprawl.

"Hey, you two. Slow down," Principal Appleberry said in her commandant voice. "You know we have speed limits in here."

The familiar "yes, ma'am" was their joint reply before they scampered through the door.

"That reminds me, Michael. You can use any of the men's or boy's room to … well, you know. And at the end of the day, you will be expected to take part in dismissal duty to help supervise the kids who take buses."

"Yes, ma'am."

"The second-grade wing is around that corner. The kids here are pretty good; no murderers that we know of. This town is not as rich as Biloxi or Jackson, so might have to help some of the kids with their supplies."

"Yes, ma'am."

"You've got superlative credentials, and you got a great referral from Ellie Atkinson. So, don't let us down." *And if Ellie Atkinson wasn't in the picture, I'd make you come to my office for some detention after school*, she thought, casting an appreciative eye his way.

"Yes, ma'am. I mean, no ma'am."

"And you can stop with all that ma'am-ing. I'm Helene. Welcome to Hernando Elementary. Remind me what your full name is again, Michael?"

"Gort. Michael Gort. But you can call me Mike."

# ACKNOWLEDGMENTS

I would like to thank the keen eyes of longtime friend and colleague Conrad Bibens for cleaning up this mess and offering insightful suggestions that made the plot come together. I would also like to thank longtime friend and colleague, Ken Ellis, for creating the cover art, and a big shout out goes to my former colleague, Loren Steffy, for taking a chance on this book. We newspaper hounds run in a pack. Lastly, I would like to thank my beautiful wife, Elizabeth, who encouraged me to get off my derriere—or on it—and write a book.

# ABOUT THE AUTHOR

Paul McGrath is an award-winning journalist and educator whose career spans five decades. He spent thirty-seven years working at the Houston Chronicle after stints in Conroe, Lubbock, and Lockhart, Texas.

McGrath graduated from Texas A&M University and earned a master's degree from Marist College. He and his wife, Liz, live on a tranquil fish-filled lake near Houston, Texas. He continues to teach at Texas A&M.

Looking for your next book?
We publish the stories you've been waiting to read!

Scan the QR code below to get 20% off your next Stoney Creek title!

For author book signings, speaking engagements, or other events, please contact us at info@stoneycreekpublishing.com

StoneyCreekPublishing.com